The Unbearable Heaviness of Stephen Seagull.

This is a work of fiction, any similarities (piggy-eyes, flatulence, living or wheezing through shit films is purely coincidental.

This is the story of a man who fits that overused term: legend. The story of a man who belongs in that select elite actually worthy of the title, up there with icons such as former Saxon bass player Steve "Dobby" Dobson, Thelma Barlow, second-from-the-left in New Kids on The Block, GG Allin, and Dean Gaffney. A man who climbed all the way from his humble beginnings at the start in Michigan to the very top of the world, stopping at the ice-cream shop on the way. A man whose destiny was clear to anyone who met him from the very start, with his potent mix of attributes that blended together to create a physical masterpiece: the speed of a cheetah, the strength of four pygmies, the sexiness of a lingerie-clad panther, the agility of a gazelle, and charisma so powerful that the authorities forced his mother to keep him hidden away in a kennel in the back garden for the first eight days of his life, just so that the rest of Michigan could get on with their lives and work, instead of wasting their time simply staring at the pudgy little fucker.

On the day of his birth it is said that a unicorn was spotted leaping over a rainbow in the sky, though the only source of this is local "character" Ketamine Joe. As our hero crawled out of his mother's battered fud, cigar clasped manfully in his tiny lips, he turned around to face her, winked coolly, and proceeded to grab a scalpel and cut his own umbilical cord. His weeping mother looked down proudly on the rugged, powerful little tot and decided to name him Stephen, after the ancient Hindu god of straight-to-DVD films.

The pair of them went home soon after, where his slightly intimidated father welcomed him with open arms. Stephen settled in quickly, and with his confident masculinity he was soon nailing things that other babies took FOREVER to learn: walking and kickboxing by the age of four months, uttering his first word ("pussy") under his breath two weeks later as he sat watching an old John Wayne western, and how to sign for his parent's deliveries from the adult websites. Stephen's father was a decent but unremarkable man, a simple Belgian-herder and part-time knee model living in a rented home. Little Stevie loved his dad, but soon decided that the life his father had chosen for himself was not going to be enough for Stephen, no way Joseph.

After an incident where baby Stephen had attempted to seduce the babysitter, it was decided amongst the three members of the family that Little Stevie was best left alone to look after himself whenever his parents went out to the bingo or dogging, and one Saturday night as he s(h)at alone, there was a knock at the door. Little Stevie waddled over, but could not reach the handle with his short, stubby little arms, being as he was a useless little twat of a baby. This quandary was quickly solved by getting the cat in a headlock until it agreed to open the door for him (I'm not sure exactly how this unlikely scene played out, but in an interview on the set of his 2008 film Deaded to Death 3, Big Stevie assured the interviewer that this was exactly how it happened, and Stephen is famed for his veracity in all matters). Standing at the door was someone who would change Little Stevie's life forever (no, not Colonel Sanders): Chinese Gary. This was the none-too-politically correct fifties, and the neighbours couldn't be arsed to try and get their tongues around the foreigner's ridiculous gobbledygook name, so they had christened him Chinese Gary, for ease of communication.

The Unbearable Heaviness of Stephen Seagull.

"Hello Stephen" said Chinese Gary. "Your parents are worried that unless they find an outlet for all of your excess energy and aggression that you will eventually turn to the dark side, and maybe try to blow up Alderaan in the future. Or past. Or whatever. To this end they have asked me to channel your potency into learning martial arts. Now I don't actually know any martial arts; your parents just assumed that being Asian I do, the racist fucknuggets. Luckily though my dad Chinese Dave, brother Chinese Bob, and mother Chinese Gertrude are all seventh Dan black belts in fourteen disciplines between them, so I'll just ask them for a hand. On Monday morning at six o-clock sharp your training begins, so I'll see you then".

Little Stevie watched this mysterious stranger walk away into the night, a stranger who would help change the direction his life was going to go in the future more than Little Stevie knew at that moment, and happily let a large watery shite fill his nappy.

The Unbearable Heaviness of Stephen Seagull.

Over the next six months Chinese Gary taught Little Stevie everything that he had half-arsedly learnt from his family the night before, and soon Little Stevie was progressing at a rapid rate. He took to it like a duck to water and was often training up to three hours a day, silently cursing the fact that Survivor's Eye of the Tiger wouldn't be written for another few decades yet, and thus couldn't be used to soundtrack his training montages (Lonnie Donegan didn't quite have the same effect when Little Stevie was punching trees and kicking the cat).

"You are coming on well, young Padawan" Chinese Gary said to him one day, after watching Little Stevie bench-pressing the paperboy for three sets of ten and finishing off with a roundhouse kick to the lad's solar plexus. "Perhaps it is time for your training to advance to the next level" he continued, as he helped the crying paperboy onto his bike.

"What do you mean Chinese Gary?" Little Stevie asked (his speech was really coming on now, and was fast approaching the vocabulary of a Gemma Collins).

"I mean that perhaps it is time for you to leave this decadent place, and travel to see someone who can elevate you to a level you truly deserve. My aunt Chinese Judith knows a man who knows a man who knows a woman who knows a man who knows a young lad who is technically not yet of an age where we can refer to him as a man but we will do for now who knows a woman, who can get us in touch with the greatest martial artist in all of Asia, and maybe even the Isle of Wight too. If he agrees and I can drag your parents away from the BDSM clubs long enough to sign an agreement, then my plan is to send you over to him and reach your true potential. What do you think about that?"

"I think I've shat myself again".

Chinese Gary let out a little laugh. "Sometimes I forget that you're still just a little twat of a baby Stevie", he said, ruffling the little fella's ponytail. "Now I'm not going to lie to you Stevie, things are going to be extremely hard for you if you do get to go over there. The master is not what you would call a friendly man, and he is an incredibly hard taskmaster. You will work as you have never worked before, which admittedly for a baby who is a few months old isn't really saying much, but he will break you down before he builds you up again, and of the twelve people he has deigned to teach over the past forty years six have died, two are confined to wheelchairs, one went stark raving mad and spends his time punching hamsters in his bedroom, and all that returned of one of the others was a shoe with a toe in it. However, the two who survived are now probably in the top ten hardest men in the world, which of course makes them the top ten hardest people in the world as women are weak, pathetic, and girly. So, are you still interested?"

"I never said I was in the first place Chinese Gary", said Little Stevie, as he picked up a ladybird and calmly popped it into his mouth. "Now are my cartoons on yet?"

Chinese Gary sighed, and picked up the chubby little shit, carrying him into the house. "Look Stevie I was trying to do this the nice way but hey ho, the truth is that your parents have gotten a little bored of you now and you're cramping their wife-swapping hobby somewhat, so they want to get rid of you by sending you across the world to some old bloke who for all I know is king of the paedos. Happy now?"

"What's a paedo Chinese Gary?"

3

The Unbearable Heaviness of Stephen Seagull.

Chinese Gary sighed again. "You know those people who introduce your cartoons on the TV every morning Stevie? Well they could probably tell you the answer to that one. Now, let's get you changed, you stinky little shit".

The Unbearable Heaviness of Stephen Seagull.

A few months later Little Stevie was on a plane to China, ready to possibly spend the next sixteen years being transformed into a granite-hewn fighting machine. There had been tears from his parents as they waved him off at the airport, but there had been none from tough little Stevie of course. As he tried in vain to flirt with the air hostesses, who for some reason didn't seem particularly interested in a sixteen-month-old child (even if he did have his own ponytail and num-chuks), he wondered what lay ahead of him in this strange country. He had once seen a cartoon set in China, but he wasn't sure how true to life it was as after all cartoons had also lead him to believe that animals can speak English, and if you drop an anvil onto a coyote from a great height he will be fine a few minutes later (something he knew from his own experimentation was false, unless coyotes are a LOT harder than next door's chihuahua).

As he sat there drinking his warm milk (the annoyingly by-the-book hostesses wouldn't give him a whisky on the rocks, much to his annoyance), the sudden thought crossed his mind that his new mentor may not even speak English! Chinese Gary and his family spoke English, but perhaps only those planning to live in civilisation bothered to learn how to speak properly, and maybe he was going to struggle to be understood over there (after all he was still just a small child, and though progressing way ahead of his peers he was still even now only at the level of a Hollyoaks actor). Ah well, he thought to himself as he drained the glass of milk (careful to flex his bicep as he did so to impress the watching hostess), trying to fathom out their primitive grunts and squeaks will all be part of the rich adventure.

Many, many, many hours and copious nappy fillings later Little Stevie landed in China, waddled carefully down the steps and into the arrivals lounge, where he had been told he would be met by a young lady holding his name written on a large cardboard sign. He scanned the crowd coolly as he strutted confidently into the throng, lollipop dangling nonchalantly from his lower lip, and only tripped up three times on the way (he's still a fuckin' BABY FFS!). He spotted a shy-looking young woman over by the toilets, with what looked like a large piece of cardboard down by her side. Presuming that this was his welcoming party (either that or she was possibly a toilet dwelling perv), he walked over.

"Hi, I'm Stevie, looking for me?"

She looked down with a start, and suddenly got very agitated and excitable.

"Where are your parents?" She said in perfect English, surprising him somewhat.

"Well as it's Tuesday night over there then they'll probably be in the middle of getting fisted by Fingers Johnny at the club."

"Bu...but you must have come over with a chaperone or someone? You're a BABY!"

He chuckled wryly. "Little Stevie don't need no chaperone babe, Little Stevie can look after himself". He gave her a cocky smile, which was undercut slightly by the involuntary fart that squeaked out of his arse immediately after.

"I need to speak to someone in authority about this" she exclaimed, looking around frantically.

"Look babe, I made it all the way from the US of friggin' A to China all by myself, I'm here now, so let's just get going and meet this great master of yours so I can begin to REALLY kick ass".

5

The Unbearable Heaviness of Stephen Seagull.

After a further ten minutes of convincing she finally relented, and lead him out to a taxi rank. They drove for what felt like hours through endless countryside, until they reached a boat at the side of a vast lake. They got into the rusty little vessel, and she began to row slowly out to an island in the middle of the lake. Once they reached their destination they walked up a small overgrown path to a wooden farmhouse, surrounded by barns on all sides. In the open doorway stood a frail, elderly Chinese gentleman, with long flowing white hair and an equally long, flowing white beard.

"Pfft" thought Little Stevie, unimpressed, I could totally kick his ass.

"So, this is the new prospect then?" Snorted the old man derisively. "He just looks like any other soft, decadent spoilt little Western brat to me. Why do you bring me such pathetic specimens of humanity and waste my time?"

I'll show this wise-ass, thought Little Stevie, and promptly dropped to the ground and blasted out twenty one-armed press-ups.

The old man snorted again, though Stevie could detect a flicker of respect flash across the old man's face for just a second, before he turned and walked back into the house.

"Bring him inside," The old man shouted over his shoulder. "Let's see what the little ball of blubber and faeces can do".

The Unbearable Heaviness of Stephen Seagull.

Those first six months would have broken a lesser man (i.e. every other man on the planet), and poor Little Stevie went to bed crying every single night like the big baby that he was. Every night he would limp slowly and carefully into the spartan bamboo bed that had been provided for him, his body a mass of purple and blue bruises. That pathetic old man was the toughest warrior that Little Stevie had met in his entire year and a bit on the planet. Many, many times Little Stevie was close to just giving in and walking out the door, and it was only his iron will and pride that stopped him from doing so. Well, that and the fact that the stumpy little twat's arms were too short to reach the oars of the boat.

Eventually though he began to see signs of real improvement in his capabilities, and as those early years dragged on he began to feel more and more powerful, agile, resourceful, and less reliant on his nappies. The master (the only title ever revealed to young Stephen) and the young woman were not exactly fascinating and outgoing, engaging company, but Stephen had to admit that both did their job brilliantly. The master was slowly turning Little Stevie into the ultimate fighting machine, and the young woman, (who handled Stevie's schooling and all other lessons in growing up to be a fully functioning human being), was an intelligent, focussed teacher (though he was becoming a little tired of her constant mutterings about the fact he should be fully toilet trained by now).

One day Little Stevie was dropkicking a calf in one of the barns when the master shuffled in, wearing a rare smile on his face (well where else was it going to be, his elbow?).

"Stephen! Come over here!"

Little Stevie delivered a final, powerful kick to the bleating calf's face, and walked over to see the master unfolding a large poster onto the floor of the barn.

"This will be your first test young man, we will see if what you have learned so far has actually sunk in yet".

Little Stevie looked at the poster, which was advertising a fighting tournament in some city he'd never heard of before.

"Do you think I am ready master?"

"You have done excellently at your training over the past few years, but the only way we can really see if it is working is in the crucible of a real fight, so I have entered you into this tournament. It is two days away, so focus!"

"Two days master? I'm not sure if I'm ready".

"Neither am I Stephen, but it is happening nonetheless. Now take that calf corpse and put it into the freezer, and then see if you can do something about stopping his mother's incessant wailing".

The Unbearable Heaviness of Stephen Seagull.

On the day of the tournament Little Stevie was excited, nervous, and a little bit dodgy in the rectal area (he was wearing a heavy-duty nappy, just to be on the safe side). He stared around constantly at the hustle and bustle of the city, a sudden shock to the system after years of the tranquillity of the farm. He had slept very little the night before, and his night nappy had been filled and changed (to much tired muttering from the woman) more than a few times with his nerve-induced diarrhoea. As he made his way to the ring he looked across and sized up his opponent, who already pacing around with a hostile look on his face. At this point in time Little Stevie was nine years old, and as he looked up at the imposing figure in front of him he guessed his opponent's age to be around fifteen, maybe sixteen. Little Stevie was probably around eleven inches smaller, give or take, and outweighed by maybe three stone. Our hero was a very confident boy, but suddenly he had an urge to fill his fresh heavy-duty nappy until it burst apart at the seams.

"CONTENDERRRRRRRRRRRRSS, RRRRRRRRREEEAADDDYYY!" The Chinese referee shouted from the centre of the ring, in a Scottish accent (for some reason).

One of the contenders was a long way from being ready at all, but he had no choice but to square up to his opponent, face to ball sack. His opponent looked down at him with a look of utter contempt, and then turned and gave a cocky little grin to an attractive young girl sitting ringside. Little Stevie tried to stop his heart from racing by reciting some of the master's favourite sayings in his head ("be as unpredictable in your movements, annoying and elusive as a fly at a picnic; fear is fuel, use it to power your fists; No matter how tall the tree is, your hand is an axe, and can chop it down to size; If in doubt, kick him in the bollocks"), but it was no use; all he wanted to do was run (and swim) all the way back to the island and crawl under his bed and hide.

The bell rang and they squared up, Stevie pondering whether he could end the fight quickly with a quick uppercut to the knee. All of his planning went out of the window when his face was suddenly rocked back by two rapid fire blows. An explosion of pain spread across his entire face, and the sudden urge to burst into tears took all of his willpower to suppress. His brain was scrambled, and it was only when he heard a Scottish voice saying "seven...eight..." somewhere above him that he realised that he must be down on the canvas. Managing to scramble back to his feet just in time, he was immediately bombarded with some more punishing blows to the head and torso. Pain enveloped his body and he could feel himself wobbling again, but he somehow managed to dodge the next few attempts to take his head off until the blessed relief of the bell sounded, and he staggered back to his corner.

Rounds two, three, and four passed in a similar fashion, and Little Stevie could see no way at all to negate his opponent's far superior size and strength. He began to curse the master for putting him in the ring long before Stevie was ready, and against an opponent so much older and larger than he was. As he reluctantly made his way back to the centre of the ring for round five, he could hear the crowd taunting and jeering, and he wished that he was anywhere but there. He threw a couple of half-hearted punches followed by a kick, but his rival was made of far sterner stuff than the chickens and piglets Stevie regularly battered back at the farm, and the only response to the blows was sarcastic laughter. Stevie threw another desperate kick towards his foe who easily evaded it, and answered in kind with a vicious kick that knocked the wind out of Stevie, and sent him slamming into the canvas once again.

The Unbearable Heaviness of Stephen Seagull.

"Ha ha" His opponent jeered, towering over Stevie's prone body. "Perhaps this fighting lark isn't for you, you stumpy little midget. Maybe you should enter the girl's competition, you twat-haired little freak".

As Little Stevie lay there on the canvas, he felt pure rage suddenly coursing through his entire body like electricity. Suddenly the pain left all the battered parts of his young body, and anger infused his previously exhausted limbs, as the sounds of the referee counting registered faintly in the background.

"SIX...SEVEN...EIGHT..."

CRACK! Blood spewed out of his rival's face as, in the blink of an eye, a furious little ball of aggression sprang up from the canvas and threw a lightning-fast punch straight into his nose. In the space of a few seconds six or seven more kicks and punches rained upon his shocked adversary, who was out for the count before his body even hit the floor. The crowd erupted in shocked cheering and applause, and Little Stevie basked in their adulation. He turned from the crowd and knelt down to the pulverised ear of his victim.

"You can punch me, you can kick me", he whispered into the still unconscious ear. "You can taunt me, you can laugh at me, but NO-ONE disses the ponytail!"

He strutted away through the crowd to the dressing room, countless hands reaching out from the crowd to pat him on the back, and entered to a warm embrace from the young teacher, and even the master gave him a satisfied pat on the shoulder. As he sat there listening to their flattery, he realised that something had changed inside him in that ring, that after beating that (relative) giant he would never fear anyone ever again; he had discovered the power of the ponytail.

The Unbearable Heaviness of Stephen Seagull.

Many years and fights passed since that life-changing debut in the ring, and eventually there came a time when Not-so-little-anymore Stevie had to return to civilisation. He was now a seventeen-year-old, and had filled out into a strapping young man. All the training had transformed the little boy into a broad-shouldered, muscular man, crowned with a magnificent black ponytail. The master and the woman had accompanied him to the airport, with the woman fighting back tears for the whole journey (Stevie assumed that she was probably in love with him). The two of them hugged in a somewhat awkward manner in the departure lounge (Stevie was trying to hide the fact that he was getting a semi), and the master gave him a firm, lingering handshake. Few words were spoken between them, but Stephen could sense the love that had grown between the three of them crackling in the air around them, and with a final smile he walked away to the plane, no longer trusting himself not to cry.

As he sat in his aeroplane seat, slyly having a quick perv at the hostess's arse, a sadness suddenly washed over him as he realised that he would probably never see the pair of them ever again. Despite the old man's grumpy demeanour and harsh treatment of Stephen a mutual fondness had developed between student and master over the years, coupled with an increasing respect as Stephen had grown into the formidable human weapon he became, and Stephen was actually going to really miss the cantankerous old fella. The woman too had opened up to him over the years, and a friendship had slowly developed during those countless lessons. Also of course, she had been the inspiration behind his first young teenage wank.

And the second, third, fourth, three thousandth, four thousandth etc.

With a start he suddenly realised that he'd forgotten to hide the crusty wanking sock left lying at the side of his bed that morning, but then figured that he was never going to see either of them again, so who cares? He settled back into the seat, looked out of the window for possibly one last time at this country he'd become so fond of over the past sixteen and a bit years, fished out a menu from the little pocket on the back of the seat in front to put over his groin, and devoted the next couple of hours to having a right good old lech at the hostess's tits n' arse.

The Unbearable Heaviness of Stephen Seagull.

He landed back in the US with the feeling of a conqueror returning. He was filled with self-belief, confident in the knowledge that he was going to make a name for himself in his homeland, and men would soon learn to quake in his presence. First though he needed to get something to eat; it had been so long since he'd tasted some good old-fashioned American junk food, and he wanted to treat himself to something he'd fantasised about for so many of those years in China, as he'd sat down to yet another bowl of fish and rice. With almost the last of the money left in his pocket that the master had given him he ordered a burger and a large Coke, and an explosion of pure delight hit his lips that instantly transported him back to a childhood spent munching into a burger in front of the TV, while his parents and Mr. and Mrs. Jones from the club made weird noises in the bedroom upstairs.

AS he sat back his chair, sate after that long-awaited treat, he thought to himself that he was really going to enjoy being back in the USA with all its culinary delights. If he was going to treat himself to the occasional burger though he would be in need of some kind of income, and with that in mind he used the last of his money he took a taxi to the roughest part of town. He figured that the quickest way for a man like him to earn a bit of cash would be to prove his aptitude in the world of war, and so headed to the part of town most likely to give him the opportunity for a fight. He walked along the rough street, past the prostitutes and drug-dealers touting for his business, his ponytail blowing majestically in the wind, until he came upon a bar. One of the windows was boarded up, and a junky was sleeping in the doorway. Stephen stepped over him and entered into the murky, dank interior. Various shady characters looked around suspiciously as he entered, and the piano player stopped playing his rinky-dinky melody for a couple of seconds, before resuming. He strode up to the bar confidently, and beckoned the barman over.

"Hi, I'm thinking that this bar might be in need of some door security, and my rates are very reasonable" (he figured he just needed to get his foot in the door at this point, and once he'd proven himself then he could start charging what he was really worth).

"No we're fine thanks, Big Dave handles all that".

"Well I'm not being funny, but he doesn't appear to be handling that very well". Stephen pointed over to a far corner, where a young hoodlum was whipping another young lad repeatedly with a Pitbull.

"He's gone for a shit, he'll deal with that in a minute".

"I can deal with it right now if you want".

"Deal with what?"

Stephen turned around to see a huge gorilla of a man dunking his hands into someone's pint, washing them, and then drying his hands on the pint owner, who sat mute, with a frightened look on his face.

The Unbearable Heaviness of Stephen Seagull.

"That incident over there, and the one over there probably needs a bit of sorting out too" Stephen replied, pointing over to where three men had stripped someone, tied them to the pool table, and were trying to pot the black into his anus (not a euphemism).

"What the FUCK does it have to do with you? Maybe I should throw YOU out of here, you interfering prick".

Stephen laughed wryly "Maybe you should try".

The gorilla suddenly lunged at Stephen but he was slow, and Stephen easily evaded the crude attack, before launching a far more refined attack of his own. In ten seconds it was all over, and the gorilla lay unconscious at Stephen's feet, as the patrons of the bar turned around and looked on, stunned.

"Holy shit!" the barman exclaimed, impressed. "No-one has ever beaten Killer before!"

"He was nothing, and not worthy of the wages you pay him. Give me his job and I'll sort out those two other problems for you right now".

"Okay, deal".

Stephen walked over, ripped the growling Pitbull out of its owner's hands, and headbutted it, knocking it out immediately. He then deftly kicked said owner in the knee, breaking it with an audible snap. His victim cried out in pain and fell down, only for Stephen to calmly pick him up again and walk to the front door, opening it with his victim's head and throwing him out onto the street. He went back, picked up the dog, and threw it out on top of its owner. He turned back and walked towards the pool table, but the three men were already backing off and grabbing their jackets, before swiftly making their exit. Stephen untied the poor bloke from the table, removed the black ball with an audible pop, and helped the man pull up his trousers. He walked back to the bar, and smiled at the barman.

"Now, let's discuss my wages". He sniffed his fingers briefly. "And is there a sink in here?"

The Unbearable Heaviness of Stephen Seagull.

Stephen soon made a real name for himself at the bar, sometimes fighting up to twenty times in one night. No matter the size of the opponent, or the times he was outnumbered, he always came out on top, and though the money wasn't great it was enough for him to rent a room at a run-down hotel not far from work, and buy himself a burger or four at the end of each shift. Things were looking up, and women were soon showing a real interest in this charismatic, ponytailed tough-guy.

One Saturday night Stephen had already had three (easy) fights, and had just sat down at the bar for a quick snack of burger, fries, shake and ice cream when five extremely large gentlemen walked in, followed by a smaller, besuited gentleman who looked very out of place in the run-down shit-hole Stephen worked. They sat down at a table, and one of the hulking brutes went to the bar. Stephen watched them with interest; they really didn't look like the kind of people who would usually frequent this establishment. As he observed the newcomers the one who had gone to the bar banged deliberately into five young men standing next to him with his shoulder, then calmly poured a pint which had been sitting on the bar over the head of the nearest one. Straight away the drenched bloke squared up to the brute, and Stephen quickly got up and strode over, burger in hand.

"Hey, come on lads, let's not do anything stupid" he said, bits of burger raining onto the faces of the six men. "I'm sure this was just a simple accident, no harm done".

"Who told you to stick your oar in?" the brute said, in a thick Russian accent. "Go back and finish your fries, before you get hurt". He gave Stephen a forceful shove in the chest, and turned back and slapped the young man hard in the face. The young lad went to throw a punch, but Stephen quickly grabbed his fist and laid a hand on his shoulder in a placating manner.

"It's okay guys, just go back to your drinks" Stephen said in a friendly manner to the group "I'll deal with this".

"Oh you will, will you?" the Russian sneered, throwing a quick, sneaky punch. Stephen ducked masterfully and threw a retaliatory uppercut, which sent the Russian crashing against the bar. Stephen followed this up with a couple of swift blows to the liver which caused the Russian to fall instantly to the ground, clutching his side. He looked like he was already done, but Stephen heard the ominous sound of chairs being scraped along the floor behind him, and turned to see the other heavies approaching with menacing looks on their faces. One of them reached Stephen first, and managed to land a couple of heavy punches on his face, but Stephen managed to slip a third and broke his opponent's nose with a vicious headbutt. With expert footwork he evaded further punches from the other men, whilst simultaneously managing to send one of them flying over a table with a thundering kick to the stomach. Another one fell down under sustained attack from Stephen's elbows, fists and feet, until there was only one left standing.

"Let's see how tough you really are" the Russian growled. He grabbed a beer bottle and smashed it on a nearby table, holding the jagged, sharp makeshift weapon up threateningly in Stephen's face.

"Give it your best shot" Stephen smirked, contemptuously.

The Russian lunged, but Stephen was too quick for him and grabbed the outstretched arm, hammering an elbow down powerfully onto it and breaking it with a sickening crack. He grabbed the Russian's head and smacked it down hard onto the table, the Russian falling to the floor, out for the count.

13

The Unbearable Heaviness of Stephen Seagull.

As Stephen looked around at his victims, lying and kneeling on the floor either unconscious or clutching their bodies in pain, the smaller gentleman got up from his seat and walked over, smiling.

"Hello Stephen" he said, extending a hand. I've heard all about you, and the stories were if anything, understated". He had an upper-class English accent, and an elegant manner.

"And who might you be?" Stephen replied, eyeing him suspiciously.

"My name is Mr. Buckingham-Windsor-Smythe, and it is a pleasure to make your acquaintance. I am a businessman with many interests in the city, and I think you would be an ideal addition to one of my most valued assets Stephen. I am always on the lookout for the highest quality of security specialist to work on the doors of my very elite nightclub Chegwins, which you may possibly have heard of".

Stephen had indeed heard of Chegwins, it was THE place to be on a Saturday night. Anyone who was anyone went there to party, and any celebrities who came to town made an instant beeline for the place. It was a vast, sprawling multi-floored nightclub, and if Stephen could get his foot in the door there then perhaps he could start to earn some decent money, and begin making some proper connections.

"Yes, I've heard of Chegwins, but I'm a little bit confused; was this" He motioned to the battered thugs sprawled around him "some kind of test?"

Buckingham-Windsor-Smythe smiled. "Yes, I wanted to see what you are made of Stephen. I want only the best for Chegwins, and I thought that the best way to test you was to see you fighting in the flesh. These were some of my best nameless rent-a-thugs, and you despatched them like swatting flies. So, are you interested in moving up in the world of hitting people?"

"Well that depends, what kind of money are we talking here?"

Buckingham-Windsor-Smythe took a notepad out of his breast pocket, wrote a figure on it, and handed it to Stephen. It was a VERY attractive offer, one he was never going to be able to resist; though he did wonder why Buckingham-Windsor-Smythe hadn't just told him, rather than writing it down. It was odd, he thought to himself, almost as though someone is scripting my life and can't be arsed to google American wages in the sixties or something. Still, he wasn't going to pass up the offer.

"Okay, you have yourself a deal sir."

Huntington-Windsor-Smythe grinned, and held out his hand "Welcome to the club Stephen".

The Unbearable Heaviness of Stephen Seagull.

It had taken Stephen an hour to walk to Chegwins for his first shift (public transport cost money, and this was something he was still a bit short of), and as he walked he noticed the gradual change in his surroundings. No longer was he surrounded on all sides by boarded up buildings, junkies, prostitutes, and mangy cats; everything here was shiny and clean. He marvelled as he approached the front of Chegwins; a huge, imposing building covered in flashing lights. He knocked on the front door, and after a few moments a large gentleman opened it and welcomed him in. He felt himself sinking into the plush carpet, and made a mental note not to let any ketchup fall from his burger. He could see stairs leading up to other floors, and bars lined every wall. The place was a sea of silver and gold, and the whole place looked spotless; unlike his old place, where even the flu virus stayed away from in case it caught something.

The large, impeccably-suited gentleman led him to an office and knocked on the door, before entering to see Huntington-Windsor-Smythe sitting at a large, opulent desk, whisky in hand.

"Ah Stephen, glad you could make it; sit down. Get him a tissue will you Thomas?"

The large gentleman, Thomas, handed Stephen a tissue, and Stephen diligently wiped the ketchup from his mouth, fingers, and lapels.

"Thank you Thomas" Stephen nodded at his (presumably) new co-worker. "It's nice to see you too Mr. Huntington-Windsor-Smythe, I can't wait to get started".

"I just wanted to go over a few things before you do Stephen, give you the lay of the land in here. Chegwins is a very different kind of establishment to that rather more earthy place you previously worked in, which I'm sure won't come as a complete surprise. You might think that there will be less trouble for you to deal with here, but you might be in for a shock; there's just a better-dressed class of thug in here sometimes. We get all kinds of the financially comfortable in here, from business tycoons, famous pop stars, to those who might perhaps be more infamous, and well-known due to their involvement in slightly more nefarious goings on, high-ranking criminals, mafia dons etc. who like to have a veneer of class and respectability, but often have the street rat mentality still bubbling not far from the surface. There is always the possibility in Chegwins that a fight you break up might result in you making some very powerful and connected enemies, do you think you can handle that?"

"I'm afraid of no man, and plastic threats run off me like ice cream off a cone, or ketchup of some fries, or raspberry sauce off some more ice cream, or gravy off a nice big roast chicken, or custard off a lovely apple tart, or"

"Yes, yes" Huntington-Windsor-Smythe interrupted, "I get the message, I just wanted you to know what you might be getting yourself into. Now we have a large team of security here, all controlled by my head of security Paul Shane. Paul runs a tight ship and takes no prisoners, so be careful around him and do as he says".

He looked Stephen up and down. "One more thing Stephen, this is a classy establishment and I like my security to reflect this, so to that end I will be providing you with a clothing budget, and tomorrow morning you will go to my tailors and get fitted up for some proper attire".

"Is what I'm wearing okay for tonight?"

15

The Unbearable Heaviness of Stephen Seagull.

"Yes, you'll do for tonight, just stand over in that dark spot by the toilets for now. Okay, take Stephen away and show him the ropes Thomas".

Thomas led Stephen back into the main area of the club, and took him upstairs. They went to a corner of dancefloor on the third floor, and approached the broad back of a seated man.

"Hey Paul, this is Stephen, the new start" Thomas said.

The man turned around and looked Stephen up and down with a look of barely concealed contempt. He was an ugly brute; long, curly black hair framing an angular, scowling face that only a drunk, desperate warthog on Viagra would possibly think about touching with someone else's bargepole.

"So this is it?" he growled, turning back to his meal, "he doesn't look like he could beat my mother, and she's been dead six years".

"I could beat your dead mother, dead grandmother and dead grandfather all on the same day, I'll beat anyone you put in front of me" Stephen replied, realising immediately that this was a pretty shit boast.

The man turned around again. "Oh yeah, and what if I put myself in front of you then?"

He got up from the table and kept rising, and rising. He must have been around 6'10" tall Stephen guessed, and almost as wide. With his heavy metal hair, build and "interesting" facial features he looked like a villain in the WWE, but Stephen was unperturbed.

"Well obviously I'd rather not fight the man in charge of me on my first day in a new job, but if you wanna go, let's go".

Paul looked him up and down, and shook his head. "Don't worry, I'm not going to batter my new employee on his first day either, which I definitely would be able to do by the way. Piss off and prove to me that you're vaguely worth the money that the boss is paying you".

He sat back down and resumed his meal, while Thomas led Stephen away to a dark remote corner of the vast room, right next to the toilets.

"Okay Stephen" he said motioning to a small, raised platform. "You stand on there so that you have a better view of what's going on, and after that it's just doing what you've already been doing at your last place but on a much larger scale. I know this might not look like the best zone in the club to have as yours, but prove yourself and who knows where you might end up. Good luck, and any problems just get one of the many bar staff to help you out, or get one of them to come and see me".

Stephen thanked him, and walked to the platform. He glanced at his watch and saw that it was ten minutes until the doors opened and his shift began, and he wondered what lay ahead of him. He pulled a Twix from his pocket, and waited for action.

The Unbearable Heaviness of Stephen Seagull.

An hour into the night and the club was already heaving. Countless members of the young and beautiful brigade streamed past him, though of course there were plenty of munters too. Music pumped and lights flashed, and the dancefloor was already packed with writhing bodies. Stephen's watchful eyes darted everywhere, eager for a chance to prove his worth to his new employees. Everyone seemed in good spirits for the moment, but he presumed that this would change as the evening wore on, and more alcohol was consumed. Quite a few young women gave him the eye as they walked past, and he realised that being on the door might be quite a good way of pulling.

"Hi, I'm Mandy, I'm one of your fellow employees; nice to meet you". Stephen looked down in the direction of the voice, to see a petite blonde smiling up at him. "Would you like me to bring you a drink or something? Staff are allowed to eat and drink what they want while they work, one of the perks of the job. Alcohol is prohibited of course".

"Hey Mandy, I'm Stephen, nice to meet you too. A glass of coke would be great thanks, and is there any chance of a couple of Mars Bars maybe? And a Bounty bar?"

"Sure Stephen, no problem".

She walked away to the bar, and he tried and failed not to look too long at her retreating arse. Having grown up on an island with only a hairy old man and one woman, his love life hadn't really begun yet (that incident with the goat in the barn didn't count).

Ok, incidents.

He decided that Mandy was going to have the honour of being his first girlfriend, and he made a plan to try and get a chance to talk further as the evening wore on. Of course if any of the many women giving him the eye should make a move on him before that then they would get first dibs; it was only fair.

Another hour or so passed before he got his first chance to prove his mettle to his new employer. He was just finishing a packet of crisps when he spotted a couple of beefy blokes pushing a skinny guy around over at the far bar. He got down off the platform and strutted over manfully, bristling with alpha male energy, ponytail glistening in the bright lights.

"Hey lads, let's chill out a bit yeah? I don't know what's happened between you but I'm sure we can settle this amicably and enjoy the rest of our night in peace".

"This dickhead barged into me and spilled my drink all over me!" the taller of the two aggressors shouted angrily.

"It was an accident, honestly" the skinny guy pleaded. "I've already apologised and offered to buy him a drink".

"Fuck that!" the tall guy shouted, "You've ruined my shirt! I'm going to take it out on your face, bitch-boy!"

He went to throw a punch, but Stephen grabbed his arm and twisted it behind his back. A sudden blow to the ear stunned Stephen for a second, but he ducked another punch from the tall guy's aggrieved

The Unbearable Heaviness of Stephen Seagull.

friend, let go of the tall man's arm and expertly grabbed his friend in a fancy wrestling type move that yet again the author hasn't bothered to research the name of.

"Ok lads that's enough, now please just leave before things move up a gear, and you get really hurt".

Tall guy threw another drunken, badly-timed and ineffectual punch which Stephen easily evaded.

"Ok, I gave you the chance" Stephen said, and promptly knocked him out with one hard punch to the face. Another blow to his friend knocked him to the floor, and although he wasn't out for the count he did spend the next minute hunting around on the floor for the two teeth that had flown out. Stephen bent down face to face.

"So, are you going to leave quietly?"

The man nodded meekly and got up to leave.

"Excuse me" Stephen shouted, "have you forgotten something?" He motioned to the tall bloke, still in the land of nod. The man returned, and with Stephen's help got his friend up onto a chair, slumped against the bar.

"Okay" said Stephen "now you are going to carry your friend out the door and get a taxi home."

"What? He's bigger than me and is a dead weight!"

"Well then maybe you should have thought about that before two of you ganged up on one man. I won't stand for any shit in my club, and the sooner that people realise this then the better. Tell you what, I'll help you get him onto your back and then off you go".

The pair of them struggled with the sleepy large gentleman, but eventually his friend waddled away with him on his back towards the door. Stephen began walking coolly back towards the platform, aware that a crowd had gathered around and witnessed the whole event. As he stood back up onto his viewpoint Mandy appeared by his side with a grin.

"Wow, that was really impressive" she said, handing him a coke. He was a little disappointed by the lack of a little snack to go along with it, but she'd learn soon enough.

"Thanks, but that was nothing; I once fought seven men when I was in Cambodia and beat them all within four minutes, and all with the broken leg I'd received rescuing children from a burning orphanage in my job working for the fire service".

"You've been to Cambodia? I'm so jealous, I haven't even left the US yet".

"Oh I've been all over the world darling, I'll have to tell you all about my travels sometime over a drink".

"Yes, I'd like that Stephen". She smiled and went back to work, and Stephen moved over slightly to the left behind a pillar, to hide the growing semi. I'll be christening that new wank sock tonight, he thought to himself with a smile.

He intervened in four more incidents over that first night, ranging from the mild to the dangerous. At the end of the shift he was tired, a little bruised, but happy with a job well done. He felt he had

The Unbearable Heaviness of Stephen Seagull.

acquitted himself well, fair when he needed to be and rough when that was the only option. As he helped the other staff checking doors, switching off lights etc. (plus the occasional shufty at Mandy's paps), he became aware of Huntington-Windsor-Smythe standing at the bar, watching him with a small smile. Their eyes met and Huntington-Windsor-Smythe walked over.

"So Stephen, how was your first night?"

"Eventful, but nothing I couldn't handle".

"Yes, I noticed that", Huntington-Windsor-Smythe smiled. "We have security cameras everywhere in the club, and as with all new starts I made it a point to keep a particular eye on you; I must say that all I'd heard about you was indeed true, and I am very impressed Stephen".

"Thank you Mr. Huntington-Windsor-Smythe, that is very kind of you. I don't suppose you have a first name I could call you?"

"No".

"Oh, okay. Well I presume I can come back for my next shift then?"

"Oh definitely Stephen, and after what I watched tonight don't be surprised if you move up the ranks in here very quickly, and we get you a better part of the club to look after very soon".

He walked away and Stephen felt a warm glow inside, only partly due to the cheese and ham toastie he'd got Mandy to rustle up five minutes ago. He was determined to make his mark on the world, and bouncing near the bogs was just the start.

The Unbearable Heaviness of Stephen Seagull.

Two months had passed and life was really coming together for Stephen: He had moved into a small but decent rented flat only twenty minutes (on the bus) from work, he was seeing Mandy regularly, he had discovered a great pizza takeaway just one street away from the flat, and he had been moved from the bogs to being one of the small group of elite door security in the club who got to watch over the main dancefloor. The only slight fly in the ointment was Paul Shane, the head of security. He was an arrogant, macho dickhead, always throwing his weight around with the staff and trying to belittle Stephen in front of them. Stephen presumed that he was threatened by the presence of another alpha male, and one with better hair. They'd had a few arguments which had grown increasingly heated, and Stephen felt it was only a matter of time before things came to a head.

Or blows.

Stephen was in the flat plucking the strings of the guitar he had bought the day before. He had always fancied learning to play, and had once fashioned a rudimentary instrument out of a large ladle and three pieces of copper wire back on the island. It had sounded completely shit, and the loudest noise came from Little Stevie's mouth when the master kicked him in the anus for ruining his favourite big spoon. Mandy was in the kitchen making his favourite snack: two mince pies in a big bap. He was really starting to develop increasingly strong feelings for her arse n' tits, and he could imagine developing a fondness for the rest of her too, over time. As he plucked away he thought to himself that he was already pretty shit hot at the instrument, and it was only a matter of time before he became a well-respected bluesman, as well as hardman. Once he started lessons there would be nothing to hold him back, unless someone tied a large piece of strong rope to the back of his belt and attached it to an artic lorry behind him, and this was a pretty remote possibility.

Suddenly the phone rang, causing a little squeak of surprise to pop out of both Stephen's mouth and anus, and he was glad that Mandy was out of the room.

"Hello?"

"Hello Stephen, how are you?" It was Huntington-Windsor-Smythe.

"I'm fine thanks boss, just chilling with my woman and my guitar".

"Excellent. Now Stephen, I have a favour to ask you. I have a friend, a very powerful businessman, who is visiting the city this coming weekend and I would like you to look after him for me. Would you do that for me? You would be paid handsomely for your time of course".

"It would be my pleasure boss".

"Thank you Stephen, I knew you wouldn't let me down. Now he does have his own security, but I've told him that there's no-one better than you Stephen, and I'm loaning you out to him to make him extra secure while he is here. This is a man with powerful enemies, so you will need to be ultra-careful. Tell me Stephen, how do you feel about handling firearms?"

"I am well versed in those boss, I worked for a while with the special forces in the Middle East five years ago, and let's just say that there are more than a few corpses buried in the desert who could testify to my skills, if they weren't dead".

The Unbearable Heaviness of Stephen Seagull.

"Five years ago? Wouldn't you have been about twelve years old then?"

"Um...well I was such a young prodigy in fighting that the special forces heard about me and requested that I join them; I am actually in the record books as the youngest member of the US special forces ever, and indeed all special forces. Unofficially of course; my mission was top secret and classified."

"Right...well anyway Stephen I'll be in touch tomorrow and iron out the finer details, speak to you then".

"Okay great boss, See you".

Stephen risked sneaking out a fart, hoping that his patented double-decker pie bonanza wasn't quite ready yet and Mandy wouldn't be returning until the smell, which reminded him a bit of rotten beef mixed with just a hint of burnt onion and egg, had dissipated a bit. He didn't want to be a bouncer for the rest of his life, even if it was in an opulent club like Chegwins, and maybe personal protection was the logical next step on his climb up the ladder. He made a mental note to look into ways to become a bodyguard in the future, and lay back down onto the bed in a relaxed and happy state, which unfortunately resulted in yet another small parp squeaking out.

"Your snack is served my lord" Mandy said as she entered the room, plate in hand. "I hope it is to your li..holy shit! What IS that smell?"

"I, er, opened the window a few moments ago and this horrible reek come flooding in, so I quickly closed it again".

"My god, it smells like a shit did a shit, then the shit that the shit did did a shit, and that shit vomited up a skunk that has lain dead on the side of the road for three weeks while passing motorists stopped and pissed on it".

"Yes, they must be working on the sewage pipes nearby or something. Anyway, thanks for the snack".

"Are you actually going to eat it in here? with THAT smell? My god Stephen, I think I've broken a nostril. I'll leave you to it". She exited the room, gagging, and Stephen merely shrugged and ate his double-decker pie bonanza with a small grin of pleasure across his face.

The Unbearable Heaviness of Stephen Seagull.

"Hello Stephen, this is Mr. Bojangles; you will be looking after him for the weekend".

The hulking Englishman motioned towards a small, elegant Italian man in his late sixties. Stephen could instantly tell that this was a man of serious power and wealth. It was early on a crisp, sunny Saturday morning, and they were standing outside the city's premier hotel, The Watery Residue. Mr. Bojangles was staying in the plush Luke Chadwick suite, a suite rumoured to cost twenty grand a week to stay in, which Stephen thought was a ridiculous amount to pay for a room in the late sixties, never mind the future, like 2020 or something. They stood out on the street in front of the hotel: Stephen, Mr. Bojangles, the Englishman, and four tough-looking dodgy foreign types with shaven heads and stylish black suits. This small group of stylish yet slightly menacing men stood beside two limos, and as Mr. Bojangles walked to the front one without even acknowledging Stephen's existence, the Englishman beckoned Stephen to follow Mr. Bojangles into the car.

Stephen got into the back, facing Mr. Bojangles, and the Englishman got in and sat beside Stephen. The other four entered the second car, and they drove away from the front of the hotel.

"So Stephen", the Englishman asked "Mr. Huntington-Windsor-Smythe had very good things to say about you, and we need and expect the best. Do you have a lot of experience in personal protection?"

"Well, I spent three years guarding a Saudi prince, taking two bullets on two separate occasions but keeping him completely safe the entire time, and I also had four months in Britain looking after a woman called Elizabeth and her husband Philip".

"Three years? You look youthful, you must have been very young to have been in such a vital and dangerous role".

"I've always been a big guy, and I've been fighting grown men since the age of six. Believe me, I wasn't too young and green for the job".

The Englishman looked sceptical, but said nothing. Mr. Bojangles looked at Stephen for a moment, and then said something in Italian to the Englishman.

"He wants to know if you are willing to give your life this weekend, if need be?"

"Tell Mr. Bojangles that I'll give my life in a heartbeat, but when I'm around the only people likely to be dying are his enemies".

The Englishman translated and Mr. Bojangles grinned at Stephen, and muttered something in his Italian gibberish. The Englishman smiled, but did not translate for Stephen.

"Where are we going?" Stephen asked, hoping there would be a tea break soon.

"That's not important for you Stephen, all you need concern yourself with is being there if we need you" the Englishman replied, staring out of the darkened window.

Conversation seemed to be over, so Stephen sat back and stared out of the window too, all the while trying to ignore the old man pissy smell coming off Mr. Bojangles.

The Unbearable Heaviness of Stephen Seagull.

After about forty minutes both cars pulled into a large industrial estate on the outskirts of town. They drove for another ten minutes past countless identical looking warehouses, until they stopped outside a nondescript looking grey warehouse, which to Stephen's eyes looked no different to any of the others. They all got out and walked into the dingy, dark interior, where Stephen noticed seven or eight figures dotted around inside, obscured by the shadows. He was glad of the gun hidden in his suit but hoped that it wouldn't be needed, especially as he had never fired a gun in his life, and wasn't entirely sure how to get the safety off. One of the figures approached and lit a cigarette, the glow lighting up a cruel, angular face.

"So, you have graced us with your presence at last Mr. Bojangles" he said in a low, menacing growl. "I hope you have brought what I asked for".

The Englishman stepped forward, subtly putting himself between the newcomer and Mr. Bojangles.

"We have brought what we consider is a fair alternative" he said, "and we hope that you will accept it with grace".

"I will only accept what I requested Mr. Smith and I've told you that repeatedly, so we may have a bit of a problem here".

"We understand that, but when you see our alternative offer then we are confident that you will change your mind and accept, even though it is not what you asked for initially".

The Englishman beckoned one of the four men who'd accompanied them over, and the man walked into the centre of the room, laying a heavy box down on the ground in front of them. He retreated back into the shadows, and the Englishman pointed to the box.

"Take a look inside please, at our very fair offer".

The newcomer looked at the Englishman, looked at Mr. Bojangles, and bent down to the box. He carefully removed the lid from the top, and peered inside. It was dark inside the warehouse and after a second or two he had to take his lighter out of his pocket to illuminate the dark interior of the box. He suddenly jumped up with a start, causing Mr. Bojangles to burst into laughter, and said something in Italian in a mocking tone.

"Now!" the Englishman shouted, and blasted the newcomer in the knee with a pistol. The four men who had accompanied them began shooting into the shadows at the other figures, who returned fire. Stephen let out a little fright-fart, but luckily it was disguised by the gunfire and no-one noticed. He leapt behind a pillar and fumbled in his suit for the pistol he had been given earlier in the day. Gunfire continued to blast all around him as he desperately groped around for the safety catch, and he flinched as a bullet pinged off the pillar near to his left ear. His legs were trembling, and he had the sudden, desperate urge to go for a piss but fought the feeling, and, steeling himself, peered around the pillar. In the murky gloom he could see a couple of their own men lying on the ground: one silent, and one whimpering like a slowly dying dog. He could see four intermittent flashes of gunfire coming from the other side of the warehouse, and just a few feet in front of him lay Mr. Bojangles on the floor, using the slumped body of the Englishman as cover. The newcomer was crawling along the floor towards him, grimacing in pain, and Stephen saw that one of the flashes of gunfire was getting nearer and nearer to

The Unbearable Heaviness of Stephen Seagull.

Mr. Bojangles each time. His heart sank as he realised that he was going to have to do something to earn his money, and also start to earn a real reputation for himself. Taking a deep breath he counted down three, two, one, in his head and jumped out from behind the pillar, blasting the gun wildly in the direction of the approaching gunfire. He must have got a lucky shot in, as the gunfire from the other direction ceased immediately, and he ran over to the crawling newcomer, who had reached Mr. Bojangles and was trying to strangle him. He kicked the newcomer hard in the face, and he released his grip on Mr. Bojangles neck and slid back down onto the ground, making strange gurgling noises as the blood from his newly-broken nose ran down the back of his throat. Stephen felt bullets whizzing past him, and turned to fire in the direction from whence they came. He heard a yell and the firing stopped, and suddenly there was silence in the air as all the gunfire halted, except for the faint gurgling coming from the newcomer. Stephen bent down to Mr. Bojangles, helping him to his feet.

"Are you okay Mr. Bojangles?" he asked, checking the old man for injury.

"Si, si" the old man answered, somehow understanding what Stephen had said, despite not speaking English. Stephen assumed that see-see must be foreign for "thank you, god-like human", or something similar. He escorted the old man out to the car, and eased him into the back seat. Stephen got into the car beside him, and told the driver to exit the premises, sharpish. He had absolutely no idea whether any of the other men who had come with them were alive or dead and he didn't care; he was being paid to look after Mr. Bojangles, and his safety was all that matters. Stephen also thought about the men he had (purely by luck) managed to shoot, and wondered whether he had killed either of them. He was shaking, and sweat lined his face, and he hoped that Mr. Bojangles didn't notice.

"Where do you want me to go?" the driver asked.

"Take us back to the hotel, I'll make a few calls".

In truth he was going to make one call, to Huntington-Windsor-Smythe, as he had not a clue who else to contact, and the old man next to him who couldn't speak a word of English wasn't going to be much help. He looked at the old man, sitting there smiling to himself, seemingly somehow quite happy with the way that things had gone, despite losing his right-hand man and possibly four employees in the course of events.

They got to the hotel and Stephen helped the old man into his suite, sat him in a chair, and then called Huntington-Windsor-Smythe.

"Hello?"

"Hi boss, it's me, Stephen".

"Ah, Stephen, so how did things go then?"

"Well Mr. Huntington-Windsor-Smythe, I'm not entirely sure. Without going into too much detail there was a bit of action and I had to get Mr. Bojangles out of there, and we're currently back in his room, minus the rest of his retinue".

"Could you put him on please Stephen?"

The Unbearable Heaviness of Stephen Seagull.

"Sure".

Stephen handed the phone to the old man, and went to the window, staring out lost in his thoughts, as the old man waffled on in Italian to Huntington-Windsor-Smythe (who presumably spoke Italian, otherwise this was going to be a really pointless and confusing phone call for both parties).

After a few moments the old man shouted something at Stephen, and held the phone out to him. Stephen took the receiver from him and spoke into the phone.

"Yes?"

"Hello again Stephen, I just wanted to tell you that Mr. Bojangles is VERY happy with the way you handled yourself today, and everything went exactly as he wanted. He has a proposition for you, he would like you to be his personal bodyguard. What do you say?"

It took Stephen by surprise, and he would have to think about it. He was a bit scared to move into a world where guns were perhaps a common occurrence, although a little excited too.

"I'm not sure boss, would you be okay with losing me from the door?"

"Stephen, I would miss you of course, but you are meant for greater things than guarding dancers in my club. If you join Mr. Bojangles you will be moving in some very exciting, influential, though often scary circles, and you will be able to make yourself potentially a lot of money. I would advise you to take his kind offer Stephen".

"Okay then boss, I'll take your advice. Could you do me a favour though and tell him? I don't speak foreign".

"No problem Stephen, hand the phone back to him and I'll see you at the club tomorrow to sort out your leaving."

Stephen gave the phone to Mr. Bojangles, and thought about this next step in his life. He would have to leave Mandy but she wasn't that great a cook anyway, and he was sure he would have no problem getting another bint in his new job once they saw his ponytail and shiny tracksuits.

The Unbearable Heaviness of Stephen Seagull.

Stephen went to the club the next day to say his goodbyes. Huntington-Windsor-Smythe was full of praise and said he was sad to see him go, and they shared a final glass of whisky together. He wrote a quick note telling Mandy she was dumped, and left it in her locker for when she started her shift later. He would miss her paps, and to a lesser extent her arse, and she wasn't a bad sort really; he hoped that eventually, over the next few years, she would be able to pull herself together and bring herself to live some kind of life again without him.

He went to the upper floor where his fellow doormen worked out in the club gym, and there followed a lot of homoerotic wrestling and hugging as they said their goodbyes. After a few minutes of this friendly banter the atmosphere suddenly changed, and Stephen turned around to see Paul Shane standing there, scowling.

"So, our little girl is leaving home" he said, a stupid grin spreading upon his Cro-Magnon visage. "Running away to the ballet Stephanie?"

"I'm actually going to visit your mother Paul, I've heard she's the cheapest whore on the whole continent, and will do ANYTHING for bottle of cheap vodka".

The grin fell from Paul's face, and he approached Stephen, fists clenched.

"What the FUCK did you just say?"

"I'm sorry Paul that was out of order, I can only apologise; I actually meant that it was your father who will do anything for vodka".

Shane swung a massive arm in Stephen's direction, and a fist the size of a hippo's head crashed into Stephen's jaw, rocking his head back and stunning him for a second. Although Paul was massive, Stephen had always slightly written him off as being much of a real threat, figuring that he was all talk and hid behind his size, but the power in that huge body shook him. He took another three or four blows to the head and body while he tried to focus again, and felt a rib crack, causing him to wince in pain. Paul spotted this and grinned, then headbutted Stephen right on the nose, resulting in what felt like another break. Stephen threw his arms around his adversary, pinning his arms to his side, to give himself some space to gather his thoughts. He struggled to hold the writhing lunk of brawn and beef, and quickly let go and sprang back into a safe distance.

"C'mon pussy" Paul said, beckoning. "I'm not done kickin' your ass yet".

Stephen shook his head to clear his mind, and blood sprayed through the air from his nose. "Warm up's over boy, now I'm ready; let's go".

They circled around each other, throwing a few exploratory punches, and Stephen struggled to keep out of the reach of his opponent's massive arms. He kept dancing around his foe, hoping to wear him out, and eventually the gorilla began to tire, his swings becoming wilder and more desperate. Stephen bided his time and then struck, landing a kick to the right knee of his opponent which brought him down nearer to Stephen's level, and following it up rapidly with three blinding punches to the jaw and cheekbone. Paul fell down onto his hands and knees and Stephen could tell he was fighting unconsciousness and was done, but he had always been a prick both to Stephen and the rest of the staff in there so Stephen wanted to make a point, and delivered a powerful kick to Shane's face, knocking him
26

The Unbearable Heaviness of Stephen Seagull.

out cold. There was silence in the gym for a moment, and then a massive cheer arose, Stephen receiving multiple pats on the back from his former colleagues, all happy to see their boss laying comatose on the floor. Stephen accepted their plaudits with grace and good humour, and then with a cheery goodbye walked out of the club to start his new adventure.

The Unbearable Heaviness of Stephen Seagull.

Many years passed, years in which Stephen became one of the world's most sought-after bodyguards, while also discovering that McDonalds had restaurants in pretty much every corner of the globe (the author, being a thick twat, wasn't entirely sure if saying that globes have corners was a stupid turn of phrase or not, but the good thing was that this bit in brackets was pushing up his word count, so he figured that it was fine to use it). He had guarded high level criminals, bankers, Middle-Eastern princes, Russian oligarchs (the only type there seemed to be), pop stars, sports stars, and every kind of person who needed someone like Stephen to protect them. He had taken a few years off in between to teach the Japanese how to fight, and felt he had done it all and eaten it all in the world of close protection. He was beginning to feel the urge to try something new, and decided that he would try and get into the world of films. He had always felt that he would make a fantastic actor, with his tall, rugged good looks, abundant charisma, fighting skills, and ponytail he was a natural for the big screen , and he felt that the time was ripe for a new action hero. To this end he had written his own script for a film: None of Them Came Back Alive, Not Even Me. It was a film set in WW2, or World War Two, as it is also known to authors constantly trying to find different ways to keep their word count up. Stephen was to play the hero (well, DUH!) Brank Hanktankerson, who faked his age to sign up and fight the Nazis at the age of fourteen. Stephen was pretty confident that he could pass for such a young age, and planned to tie his boots to his knees and kneel down for the duration of the film. His moving yet action-filled story showed the blossoming of a young man, ponytail still in its infancy, into an awesomely heroic leader of men, culminating in a grand finale where Stephen takes on and defeats four tanks armed only with a packet of Hubba Bubba, all to save his best friend Dumpy Rustynuts.

Stephen was confident that the script was a winner, and all he needed now was to get it under the noses of the right people. Luckily for him his current job was guarding the owner of Patriot Films, the largest film company that you've never heard of in the world (at that time. In a very specific part of the world. Depending on the time of day).

Mr. Johnstone was a corpulent gentleman who always dressed in Hawaiian shirts and shorts, topped off with a pair of sunglasses permanently attached to his face. He was a self-made millionaire who loved action films, and luckily for Stephen he had taken a real shine to his new bodyguard. They were on the set of the company's latest film, War Hippo, and Mr. Johnstone seemed uncharacteristically subdued.

"Anything wrong boss?" Stephen asked, handing him a cool glass of water.

"Oh nothing really Stephen, just a feeling that we're not seeing anything new here, it's just the same old action film we've been doing for a few years now, albeit with a special forces hippo going undercover as a spy into Nazi Germany in this one. I need something new, something fresh".

Stephen grinned.

"Well it's funny you should say that boss" he said, reaching into a carrier bag by his side. "I've written a little something here that you might like".

He reached into the bag and brought out his dog-eared script, handing it to Mr. Johnstone.

Mr. Johnstone had a read of the synopsis written at the front.

"So it's about a war hero then".

The Unbearable Heaviness of Stephen Seagull.

"Yeah."

"Why is that any different to War Hippo, Tankstrangler, Gutpunisher 3, or Ears of Fury?"

"Um, he has a bit of a ponytail".

"I'm not convinced Stephen".

"Look, please Mr. Johnstone, just give it a chance and read it; I'm sure you'll change your mind".

"Okay then Stephen, since it's you I'll give it a fair trial".

"Thanks Mr. Johnstone, and apologies for the chocolate stains".

For the next two days Mr. Johnstone never even mentioned the script, and Stephen was beginning to think that he hadn't even bothered to read it. He was beginning to feel a bit down, but then on the third day Mr. Johnstone greeted him heartily on set, hugging him and slapping him repeatedly on the back (which got a bit annoying, if Stephen was honest).

"Stephen! This script is fantastic! We are going to make a lot of money from this my boy!"

A massive grin spread across Stephen's relieved face. "That's great boss, I'm so happy you like it".

The smile faltered for a brief moment on Mr. Johnstone's face, replaced by a concerned look.

"Stephen" he said, laying a paternal hand on his bodyguard's shoulder. "there's just one slight problem I have with it, and that's the fact that you have written yourself in as the lead character. You haven't acted before, have you Stephen?"

"Well actually boss I toured for seven months in the Royal Shakespeare Company's production of The Taming of the Shrew over in Saigon when I was in my late teens, and earned the country's equivalent of a Tony award, a Big Bert for my performance".

Mr. Johnstone looked surprised, then smiled again. "Oh I didn't know that Stephen, excellent news! Do you really think you can pull off acting as a fourteen-year-old boy though?"

"No problem boss, leave it to me".

"Great, we'll finish up with War Hippo and then I'll start looking for a director and cast etc. for the film; you're gonna be a movie star Stephen!"

Stephen smiled back, already imagining his Oscar speech after the voting panel sees the scene where he cradles Chugger Bronksteiin in a bomb crater and slowly soothes him into death, gently serenading Chugger with Whitesnake's Here I Go Again on an acoustic guitar as he slips away (a song which didn't exist in WW2, sorry, World War Two, but Stephen figured that the general public were thick fuckers, and wouldn't notice).

The Unbearable Heaviness of Stephen Seagull.

A month later and filming had begun on None of them Came Back Alive, Not Even Me, and Stephen was excitedly attaching a pair of boots to the front of his knees. He had (reluctantly) cut his ponytail right back, and was sure that he could pass for fourteen. Patricia Bouffant had been cast as the love interest, a German prisoner who hates Brank initially, but falls in love with him just in time for the credits (the fact that Brank was fourteen and she was twenty-eight was a little bit problematic, but Stephen assumed that they didn't give a shit so much about that kind of thing back then, and Stephen was only PLAYING a fourteen-year-old; he was now thirty three, so it shouldn't matter). Patricia was a rising soap actress, famous enough to be a bit of a draw, but unknown enough to get on the cheap. The rest of the cast were unknowns, but Stephen figured that with a story this strong that wouldn't remain the case for very long.

He looked in the mirror, and was pleased with what he saw. Okay, the boots hanging off his knees looked a little bit silly, but once he was on set and down on his knees, then he would look perfectly normal as a fourteen-year-old-sized soldier. He strode out into the sunshine and walked towards the set, eager to start kicking ass as an actor.

Patricia was already there, surrounded by the other, lesser actors and extras, all eager to bask in her minor star-wattage. Stephen chuckled as he approached, knowing that once he appeared on the scene that all the others would fade from her view, and she would be captivated by this handsome stranger with boots on his knees.

"Hello Patricia, I'm Stephen, the writer and main star of this feature, nice to meet you".

She turned around, blond curls swishing around her head like in a shampoo commercial, and smiled. "Hello Stephen, nice to meet you too. I can't wait to get started, this is my first film; hopefully the first of many".

"It's the same for me Patricia, and I'm sure that we both have a great future in film ahead of us". He wasn't entirely sure if this was true as he had seen the soap she starred in, and she had frequently been out-acted by her sandwich. However the soap and she were inexplicably popular, and it made good business sense to use her for the film. "Shall we begin?"

That first day of filming went swimmingly, and Stephen took to it like a duck to water. The other actors and extras were instantly in awe of this natural actor (he assumed), and Patricia was falling in love with him already. The director was some journeyman from Spanish TV, but Stephen was confident that the quality of the script and his own overwhelming charisma and talent would ensure that the film was a success. He hadn't been paid a fortune for the script, and nor was he getting the kind of leading man wages that a man of his stature deserved, but he knew that it was only a matter of time before the money and adulation began pouring in. He had asked Patricia if she fancied having a drink in his trailer after they had finished for the day, but she said that unfortunately she had to arrange her pot plants into alphabetical order, and wouldn't manage. It was a shame, but there would be other nights, and at least it meant that he didn't have to share his fudge cake.

The Unbearable Heaviness of Stephen Seagull.

The film was finished on schedule and released to decent reviews ("Watchable pish"-The San Francisco Herald; "I was awake for most of it"-The London Bugle; "The seat in the cinema was very comfy"-Tokyo Film and Swimwear Magazine; "You see a bit of side-boob at around the hour mark"-Financial Times), and making a surprisingly healthy profit. Johnstone immediately handed Stephen a contract tying him to do five more films, and they went straight into filming Stephen's second script: Satan's Kestrel. In this Stephen would be playing troubled mercenary Bronston Masticator, hired to kill a female woman whose testimony can put away a top mafioso for a very long time. Inevitably she falls in love with Bronston, and he is torn between doing his job or saving the woman who loves him.

Stephen had hoped to rehire Patricia as he still hadn't quite managed to pull her, somehow, (she had always been busy, frustratingly, whether it was ironing her scripts, polishing her knitting needles, checking the dampness of the water in her kettle, weighing her underwear, or stroking her pens, she always seemed to have to do something she needed to do whenever he asked her for a drink),but she had to film a special Christmas episode of her soap. Instead he had turned to Susan HolstenWeissein, a veteran of many Patriot films including Fist of Orkney, Kill Slay Kill 3, Ghost-dog of the Somme, and The Beast From Another Wardrobe. She wasn't really to Stephen's taste, but he would probably pull her anyway just to keep her happy, and the rest of the cast and crew he already knew as they had worked on the first film (many would be wearing wigs or glasses so it wasn't TOO obvious that it was almost exactly the same bunch of people in both films).

The scene they were filming that afternoon was one where Bronston had been captured by the mafia and was being tortured in an underground basement. Susan wasn't in the scene, but he had let her watch it, just so she could see how cool he was.

"So, why don't you tell us where Miss Underwood is, it will save you a lot of pain" one of the henchmen said in a thick Italian accent, leaning into Bronston while brandishing a large knife.

Bronston chuckled scornfully, and looked his adversary straight in the eye with a mean stare. "I eat pain for breakfast, and shit agony motherfucka".

"Oh, do you have piles?"

"No, only piles of weapons stashed away ready to blow your frickin' heads off" Bronston added coolly, all the while fumbling with the ropes that tied him to the chair.

All five mafioso burst into Italian-accented laughter, before the main henchman leant back into Stephen's face, the smile slowly fading from his slab-like face.

"For a man strapped to a chair, slashed multiple times already and beaten black and blue, you are strangely confident". He turned around to an accomplice. "Get the tools out, I think that it's time we stepped this up a level".

Bronston faked a large yawn, and pretended to be sleepy. "Wake me when you're finished with this torture then, maybe we can have pancakes once you're finished".

The accomplice walked forward holding a chainsaw, hammer, jar of Marmite and a pelican on a leash, and uttered something in Italian to the main henchman.

The Unbearable Heaviness of Stephen Seagull.

"My friend here says that pancakes are far more enjoyable to eat when you still have teeth, a tongue and lips. Now, I am going to get very creative over the next five hours, and you are going to tell me where Miss Underwood is, or you will wish that you were dead".

"Won't telling you be a lot harder without lips and a tongue?"

"...JUST SHUT UP!"

He revved up the chainsaw and advanced towards Bronston with a leer, as he raised it above his head he made the mistake of looking around and muttering something in Italian to his colleagues, and Bronston took this chance to launch himself at his tormentor, having successfully freed himself from his bonds. With a tremendous punch both the chainsaw and its handler went flying in opposite directions, and Bronston expertly caught the chainsaw in mid-air and threw it straight through one of his torturers, cutting him into two parts (the chainsaw wasn't actually on, and the noise if it running was a stuntman standing off camera shouting "RRRRRR-N-N-N-N-N-NING-NING-NING, RRRRRR-N-N-N-N-N-NING-NING-NING", but the director assured Stephen that it would look realistic on camera). Bronston quickly knelt down and removed the laces from his boots, fashioning them into a lasso and roping another of the baddies round the neck and hoisting him over the rafter of the roof, hanging him instantly. He grabbed the chair from behind him and threw it at another baddie, whose head broke of its neck as the chair hit it at full force, and rolled away into the corner where it landed upright, a look of shock still on its stupid dead face. Two of the remaining three thugs began to draw their guns but Bronston was too quick, and jumping up into the air he kicked them both in the face, sending them flying back and onto the horns of two Rhino heads hanging on the wall (trophies from the owner's hunting trip to somewhere in Africa; Stephen couldn't be bothered to research what countries in Africa rhinos actually lived), impaling them and killing them instantly.

Bronston walked over and picked up the leash of the pelican, walking slowly over to the main henchman, who was still lying groggily on the floor.

"Now it's my turn to indulge in a little torture" Bronston said with a sadistic grin, brandishing the pelican threateningly.

Aaaaaaaaaaaaand...cut.

Everyone on set whooped and cheered, the scene had gone brilliantly, and the director bounded over, patting Stephen on the back excitedly.

"That was brilliant Stephen, so realistic!" He gushed, as Stephen bowed to his adoring worshippers. He looked over at Susan who gazed back at him in pure lust, though of course she was trying to play it cool by not actually looking at him at all and chatting to an extra, but Stephen could read between the lines. If there was one thing he knew, it was women. And the price of a Big mac in over forty countries. Okay that was two things, but the point stood. Stephen had a great feeling about the film, and was pretty confident that it would build on the (minor) success of the first film, and break him as the next major action star. He knew that he was meant for better things than the Patriot company, who were great in some ways, but not the premier league company that a man of his calibre deserved. Still, this would come as sure as eggs is eggs and chips is chips, and ham is ham and sausages is sausages, and crisps is crisps, and cheese toasties is cheese toasties.

The Unbearable Heaviness of Stephen Seagull.

He walked over to Susan and stood between her and the extra she was talking to, "accidently" standing on the extra's toes and giving him a small nudge with his elbow. The extra took this subtle hint and fucked off, and Stephen picked up a sausage roll from the catering trolley and smiled at Susan.

"Great scene eh?"

"Yeah…it was certainly…unique, I'll give you that…um…Stephen?"

"Yes, Stephen. I presume you're looking forward to our love scene?"

"Well that's about four weeks away Stephen, I've not really thought about it yet to be honest. I'm looking forward to my first scene tomorrow though".

"Yeah, that should be good. I was thinking though, in our love scene maybe there should be some tasteful nudity from you, nothing gratuitous of course, just a flash of baps and maybe a very subtle hint of minge".

"I have a STRICT no nudity clause in my contract Stephen and there will be NO nudity of any kind, thank you very much".

"Okay, we can get back to that at a later date. Maybe just an arse shot or something, but to be discussed. Anyway, I was thinking that the lingerie would be better red rather than the black I originally envisaged, and when you come out of the shower the towel might for plot reasons be very brief, and not quite cover your cheeks completely".

She shook her head in disgust, and walked away to her trailer. Stephen took out a notepad and flicking to some notes, wrote "no verbal objection" next to the "lingerie-red?" note scribbled therein. He went over to his own trailer, his pockets stuffed with sausage rolls from the catering trolley.

The Unbearable Heaviness of Stephen Seagull.

Two weeks later Susan had left the project for some luvvie, up-her-own-arse reason, so they had to quickly re-shoot some scenes with a hastily cast replacement: Angie Woodward, a young starlet just starting out in the world of acting. This actually turned out to be a good thing for the film, as not only was she willing to work for a far smaller rate of pay than Susan the diva, but she was also prepared to do the integral-to-the-plot nude scenes, which ended up lasting a lot longer due to a sudden burst of writing inspiration from Stephen. Stephen ended up humping her for the duration of the film, though of course she had wanted their fling to last beyond that. Stephen had kindly explained to her though that he was soon to be a very big star and so would be out of her league, and deserving of someone quite a bit sexier.

Satan's Kestrel opened to reviews every bit as strong as the first film ("lovely shoes"-Boston Empire; "the equal of the first film"-The Singapore Review; "the words were spoken in the correct order"-Los Angeles Butcher and Candlestick Maker magazine), and soon Stephen's name was being spoken about the length and breadth of the small apartment complex where he lived. He was now the biggest star at Patriot Films, blessed with all the luxury that entailed: his own SodaStream in his trailer; his own teacup; one of those chairs with his name on the back of it; a litre jug of the third-best shampoo in Peru; and first pick of the cute extras. He rattled through the scripts for his next four films at a fevered pace: The Moped Mauler; It Came from Outer Mongolia; Genghis Khan Kick Your Ass, and The Hurtinator, each one making a profit and adding to his fame and bank balance. Of course the inevitable happened and Hollywood came sniffing around, and with a heavy heart Stephen said his goodbyes to Mr. Johnstone and headed to LA to film his first project for one of the majors: The Stabby Gun. Again he had written it himself and based it on his own life, detailing the time that he'd saved Frank Sinatra from forty-seven bazooka-wielding Vietcong back when they were both in 'Nam. With this production he was now in the big leagues, and he could finally get a cast worthy of going toe-to-toe with him. He assembled some of the biggest names in action to act alongside him as his brigade: Kurt Wrangler, Hank Brannigan, Steele Foxxton, Billy Kronk and Coney Marsden all signed up, along with three or four lasses with tight dresses n' that.

With real money behind him to promote his films Stephen just knew that he was now going to be THE action star of the decade, and now that his ponytail was back to full strength there was no stopping him. He had also formed a blues band now he was in LA, blowing away crowds sometimes numbering up to thirteen with his soulful guitar playing and perfunctory vocals. The thought crossed his mind that as he was equally great at this as he was at acting, then maybe he should pursue a full-time career in music, but he figured that he could always go back to it once he was too old to fight on film, say when he was about eighty or so. Those gold and platinum albums would just have to wait.

The Stabby Gun opened strongly, and did far better in the international market than his previous films, though some sniffy reviews questioned the veracity and realism of the storyline. Kill Him with His Own Blood, Say Hiya to Hell, Testicles of the Jaguar, and Samurai Henry followed soon after, continuing his amazing run of success. He decided that now it was time to unleash the film he was convinced was to be his absolute masterpiece: Trapped on a Big Ship, the story of a former special forces leader now working as a chef on a pleasure cruiser, who foils a ransom attempt by a bunch of armed-to-the-teeth madmen. He was sure that with its blend of stunning action, eccentric baddies, and naked tits flopping out of birthday cakes, that the film was going to be a huge success.

The Unbearable Heaviness of Stephen Seagull.

He had let the bodyguard business go dormant while he concentrated on his acting and screenwriting skills, but he was still involved with the more violent side of things in his real life, telling his new powerful friends all about his role in helping the SAS, SBS, and Navy Seals learn how to fight properly, plus of course some stuff he wasn't allowed to reveal, for reasons of national security. There were times while playing with his band that he would have to act as his own bouncer, throwing rowdy drunks out with one hand while playing a blistering solo with the other, and all to rapturous applause from Gary, the crowd. Yes, life was looking almost as good as he was, though not quite as chubby.

The Unbearable Heaviness of Stephen Seagull.

Trapped on a Big Ship was a massive hit, and Stephen was now the talk of the town (Skegness). Women were throwing themselves at him, men wanted to be him, and dogs wanted to sniff him. Getting-A-Bit-Chunky-There-Stevie had finally made it, and he was going to enjoy the ride. Money began pouring in, And Getting-a-bit-Chunky-There-Stevie splashed out on a vast bachelor pad, sports cars, a private jet, and a range of expensive bespoke suits with elasticated waistbands. Trapped on a Big ship 2 followed and though not as successful it still did reasonable business, keeping Getting-A-Bit-Chunky-There-Stevie at the top of the acting world, where he (felt he) belonged.

He rattled through a slew of films over the next few years, eager to strike while the iron was hot, but unfortunately his star had begun to fade as quickly as it had risen. Mean, jealous critics said that this was because he was a pish actor with piggy eyes and an ever-expanding girth whose films all looked the same, but this was clearly nonsense as One-Man Army, Lone Warrior, I Used to be in the SAS But Now I'm a Humble Taxi Driver, Standalone Brannigan, and Karate Machine: He Fights by Himself, were all very different films. Yes, in these films Getting-A-Little-Bit-Chunky-There-Stevie tended to play men who wandered alone into strange new towns and end up fighting multiple baddies to save a poor widow being harassed to sell the family farm to evil land developers, and yes, the baddies tended to be either English or Russian no matter where the film was set, But in Standalone Brannigan for instance his character wore a hat, and in Angry Professional Saxophonist With a Secret the baddies were from the Middle-East. The critics were just bitter, envious nobodies who were disappointed with the way their life had gone, and didn't want to be reminded of what success really looked like by the likes of Getting-A-Little-Bit-Chunky-There-Stevie. He wasn't worried though, and knew that eventually things would come good again, and people would remember how fantastic and hard he was and start watching his films again, and not just on some obscure TV channel on a Thursday evening when they were flicking through the channels and there was fuck all else on.

Now in his mid-forties, some argued that he couldn't really pull off the tough guy roles anymore, and that seeing someone of his generous proportions fighting hordes of men half his age and beating them was a bit comical, but they were wrong about this and he was right. He had signed a deal with a smaller, but still influential and respected (probably) film company Du Beke Productions, and was confident that his new film would get him back on top. Angel of Chaos was to be his first self-penned film in a good few years; Getting-A-Little-Bit-Chunky-There-Stevie deciding that part of the reason for his declining success rate in recent times had been relying on other writer's scripts instead of trusting his own talent. Only he knew how to write a real kick-ass film, not those Hollywood Nancy-boys who had probably never been in a fight or worked as an undercover assassin in Afghanistan for four years in their lives.

Angel of Chaos was the story of a young single mother who lived in a rough neighbourhood with her disabled daughter, living close to breaking point. Her daughter is always being robbed on the way home from school by the gangs and drug dealers who roam the streets, and the mother is being illegally pressured by property developers to sell her home for a minimal fee, property developers not averse to using violent and intimating measures to get the results they want. One night, in an incredibly moving scene that caused even tough-guy Getting-A-Little-Bit-Chunky-There-Stevie to weep a little (in a rugged, manly and powerful way), the mother, at the end of her tether, falls into despair and takes an overdose, desperate to end her unrelenting suffering. As she fades gently into unconsciousness, she says a heartfelt prayer to God to take care of her daughter for her, and her tear-stained eyes close, resigned to

The Unbearable Heaviness of Stephen Seagull.

her fate. She awakens sometime later alone in a hospital ward attached to a drip, alone that is except for a large, powerful being standing at the foot of her bed, a being with large white wings sprouting out of its back, and bullet belts crisscrossing the torso and with a machine gun in either hand. Getting-A-Little-Bit-Chunky-There-Stevie is the Angel of Chaos, sent by God to kick ass on, and right a few a wrongs in the local neighbourhood.

Filming took place over a tight three weeks, and the budget was about the same as had been spent on the catering alone on the set of Trapped on a Big Ship, but Stephen was confident that the quality of the film would overcome such small hardships. The budget couldn't be stretched to hire the special effects bloke he wanted, so they had to make do with a couple of geese wings stapled to the back of a bomber jacket for the angel's look, and five interchangeable thugs had to wear a variety of wigs, false teeth, sunglasses, and different t-shirts to look like there were loads of different baddies. Getting-A-Little-Bit-Chunky-There-Stevie had also managed to procure some second-hand shop mannequins, which he arranged in the background of scenes in deliberately murky lighting to give the illusion of more gang members. Unfortunately the budgetary constraints also meant that he couldn't afford to hire baddies AND an actress to play the young mother, so he chose the shortest, slenderest thug and put him in cheap dresses and a wig, and filmed all of "her" scenes from behind, or very far away. This also meant that in certain scenes the thug had to utter "her" lines in a girly voice, and then crawl under the camera's line of view and pop up at the other side with a hastily thrown on "bad-guy" outfit, and threaten "her" in a gruff baddie voice.

Getting-A-Little-Bit-Chunky-There-Stevie would further save money by doing the soundtrack himself, his tasteful blues guitar playing majestically over the pre-recorded beats from his Bontempi organ. When it was all wrapped up even Stephen, normally his own harshest critic, thought that it was probably one of the top four films of all time, with a lead actor the equal of Olivier, Brando, Poitier, Rickitt, De Niro and a couple of chick actors thrown in so as not to look sexist. He pulled out all the stops to promote the film: doing the rounds of all magazines and newspapers from here to a bit further over there, and appearing on every chat show that would pay his fuel costs and provide a few sausage rolls in the green room.

Angel of Chaos opened to his strongest reviews in years ("it will be good when it's finished"-The Glasgow Parsnip; "what was that other shit film he was in again, the one with the killer pigeon? It's on a par with that"-The Sussex Film and Television Magazine; "I used to have a Bontempi when I was little, happy memories…"-The Madrid Echo) and had a strong opening weekend (in a part of Brazil, one of the jungly bits), but unfortunately it soon began to slip down the charts and went the way of all his other recent films. Getting-A-Bit-Chunky-There-Stevie began to get really despondent at the lack of intelligence and taste in humanity nowadays, and was increasingly resigned to the fact that his ouevre, ovreau, body of work would probably only be appreciated as the art that it is in the future, but this was cold comfort in the meantime. He decided that it was time to take a break from Hollywood, that it was time to go on a spiritual journey elsewhere in a bid to find himself. It shouldn't be too hard, with that belly.

The Unbearable Heaviness of Stephen Seagull.

Getting-A-Little-Bit-Chunky-There-Stevie landed in Moscow and was immediately struck by how cold it was. When he had left the US it had been the height of summer, and standing there in the snow in his Speedos and flip-flops he immediately regretted not getting changed for the flight. He had clothes in his suitcases though so It wasn't really a problem, as long as he made it to the hotel without dying of frostbite to the testicles first.

He had decided to go to Russia on his sabbatical as that was where most of the baddies seemed to come from (in film and therefore in real life), so he figured that there must be a lot of people wanting to learn self-defence from a master like him. He had informed his agent of the hotel's contact details in case any really good offers came in, but his agent had told him to relax and enjoy his little rest and anyway, his agent was really busy at that moment with his other full-time job at the laundrette, so wasn't always home to take calls anyway. He went to the hotel and changed into something more suitable (shiny tracksuit with a big jumper on top), when the phone rang.

"Hello?"

A Russian voice babbled in incomprehensible Russian.

"Speak normal please, you make no sense".

"Sorry, this is reception" the voice said, in faltering English. "I have someone on the other line for you".

For me? Thought Getting-A-Bit-Chunky-There-Stevie, my agent must have gotten a really good offer already. Typical, I take time off and Scorsese wants me to play the lead in his new blockbuster epic about the Malta mafia.

"Put Mr. Scorsese through".

"Um…I don't know who that is, but I'm connecting you now".

After a moment another Russian voice came onto the line. "Hello Mr. Seagull, I hope I find you well? First of all may I extend a warm welcome you to our fine city and country. I represent a man called Vladimir Putin, who you may have heard of. Mr. Putin is a huge fan of yours, ever since watching the Bear-Fighter box set as a younger man. He would like to invite you to meet him; at your convenience, of course".

This was amazing, the leader of Russia at that time (the author hoped, not being arsed again to do any research whatsoever into timelines n' that) wanted to meet him! If the leader of Russia was a fan then by extension then everyone else in Russia must be a huge fan of him too, he thought with impeccable logic. The Russians must really be ahead of the rest of the world in the field of the arts and beating people up, and maybe he had finally found his spiritual home after all this time.

"That would be an honour, I would be humbled to meet such an illustrious leader of men, and I would be happy to see him whenever it is suitable for him ".

"Excellent, that is fabulous news Stephen, I will find out what is a good time for him and get back to you at this number, and I thank you for your time".

"No, thank you sir, goodbye".

38

The Unbearable Heaviness of Stephen Seagull.

Getting-A-Bit-Chunky-There-Stevie sat down on the bed with a satisfied grin on his face, as well as a bit of an old man grunt. Things were looking up for him in Russia already, and he hadn't even beaten anyone up yet!

The Unbearable Heaviness of Stephen Seagull.

"Hello Stephen, this way please".

Getting-A-Bit-Chunky-There-Stevie followed the sombre Russian aide along the plush hallway, until they reached a solid-looking wooden door. Despite being a handsome, virile, hard-as-nails legend, Getting-A-Bit-Chunky-There-Stevie felt a little nervous now that he was actually here to meet the great man. He had put on his best shiny tracksuit and brushed his ponytail over and over, eager to make a good impression and represent the USA well.

The door creaked open slowly and a gong sounded as they entered a vast red and black room. At the far end stood a large gold raised platform, with steps going up the front that lead to a large plush velvet and gold throne. Chains attached to the arms of the throne led down to the sides, and on the ends of these chains sat two large, powerful white tigers, eyeing Getting-A-Bit-Chunky-There-Stevie impassively. Behind the throne on either side stood two tall cages, and inside danced two nubile and naked young strumpets. The room was dimly lit except for two spotlights shining down directly onto the throne, wherein sat the man himself: Putin, in a black silk dressing gown and with a tastefully diamond-encrusted gold crown perched upon his head. He beckoned Getting-A-Bit-Chunky-There-Stevie to ascend the steps towards him, and held out his hand for Getting-A-Bit-Chunky-There-Stevie to kiss. Getting-A-Bit-Chunky-There-Stevie hesitated for a moment, wondering if this was an acceptable thing for someone as incredibly heterosexual as he was to do, but then gave in and graced the outstretched hand with a (very) quick peck.

"Hello Stephen, it is amazing to meet me".

"Yes, I am a big admirer of you Vladimir". This wasn't entirely true, Getting-A-Bit-Chunky-There-Stevie was a bit clueless when it came to world politics (and his home country of the USA was part of that world). All that he really knew about Vladimir Putin was that he was the leader of Russia, and his name was Vladimir Putin.

"I am a great admirer of you too Stephen, I have all of your films in my collection".

"Thank you Vladimir, may I ask what your favourite is?"

"Yes, you may".

"Um, okay, which is your favourite of my films?"

"Well Stephen, I love all of your films, but if it had to pick a top five it would probably be Gusset of Valour, Punching Argentina, Hard Squad Five, Machine-Gun Meg, and Tankfist Maclure, though ask me again tomorrow and that would probably change. I love how varied your films are, with different types of punches and different types of kicks in many of them. I am very tough myself of course, being a black belt in judo and the toughest of all the world leaders, no question".

"Oh I have no doubt about that Mr. Putin sir, though if you would like to be even tougher then I would be more than happy to give you a few lessons; free of charge of course".

"I don't really need it to be honest but I will accept your kind offer Stephen, and would love to have a little sparring session with you. You have enjoyed your time with me but for now time is up, and you may leave". He waved Stephen away, and the spotlights above him went out, leaving the room in almost

The Unbearable Heaviness of Stephen Seagull.

total darkness. Getting-A-Bit-Chunky-There-Stevie fumbled around in the darkness, until the hand of the aide gently grabbed his elbow and led him to the door. Once out in the hallway the door creaked shut behind them, and the aide took Getting-a-Bit-Chunky-There-Stevie out into the cold air outside.

"We will be in touch with you to arrange a training session Stephen, and we thank you for coming".

"No problem, I look forward to hearing from you again".

The aide ushered him to a waiting car, and Getting-A-Bit-Chunky-There-Stevie was driven back to the hotel, feeling that a real bond had developed between these two alpha males.

The Unbearable Heaviness of Stephen Seagull.

After a couple of days of seeing the sites and buying Scarves, hats and mittens, Stephen was finally summoned for the sparring session. A car picked him up and drove him for what felt like hours out of the city, until they came to a log cabin in the middle of a dense, snowy forest. They got out, and the driver led him over to the log cabin. Inside it was cold and spartan, with nothing to see except a table with two bottles of vodka sitting atop, and what looked like a large furry nappy lain out next to them.

"Undress please, and put that on" the driver said, gruffly.

"Um... what?"

"Put it on!"

Getting-A-Bit-Chunky-There-Stevie looked at him for signs of it being a joke, but that impassive face brooked no quarter. Getting-A-Bit-Chunky-There-Stevie looked at the large pistol strapped to the driver's front and the grenades hanging off his belt (which Getting-A-Bit-Chunky-There-Stevie had thought was a bit much for a glorified taxi driver accompanying a willing tourist), and decided that perhaps it was for the best to comply. He stripped, muttered "it's very cold in here, isn't it?", and donned the furry nappy. Once done the driver led him back outside into the snowy landscape, and Getting-A-Bit-Chunky-There-Stevie felt his genitals pull up into his throat. The pair of them went around the back of the cabin (Chunky and the driver, not Chunky's testicles. Though they came too.) to see Putin already there, equally naked except for the same (albeit smaller) furry nappy. He was circling around doing martial arts moves, and grinned when he spotted Getting-A-Bit-Chunky-There-Stevie.

"Hey, Stephen, so glad you could make it! You look very manly in your bearskin, and congratulations on such perky nipples".

"Um, thank you Mr. Putin" said Getting-A-Bit-Chunky-There-Stevie, his teeth chattering as he spoke.

"This is the way that true men fight in Russia, none of your weak Western decadence for us! Now oil yourself up and join me".

Getting-A-Bit-Chunky-There-Stevie looked around, and the driver motioned to a large open drum of thick looking liquid. Getting-A-Bit-Chunky-There-Stevie stood there for the next few moments feeling awkward, as the driver slathered copious amounts of greasy liquid all over his body. It was particularly awkward as Getting-A-Bit-Chunky-There-Stevie was A) trying to stop from shivering in case the driver thought he was indeed a weak Westerner, and B) trying to quell the semi he could feel rising in his furry nappy.

"Come Stephen, wrestle me!" shouted Vladimir, beckoning him over.

What followed was three hours of the most awkward, weird, exciting, sexually-confusing, freezing, and slippery action that Getting-A-Bit-Chunky-There-Stevie had ever indulged in. At a few points he thought that he had felt something hard poking him through his opponent's furry nappy, but as he himself had quickly given up on trying to disguise his tumescence he relaxed about it all, and realised that this was merely two strapping, powerful, almost-naked athletes getting a bit excited at such an overpowering display of ultra-masculine heterosexual power. No woman could resist this, he had thought at one point in proceedings, as their pasty, flabby middle-aged bodies slapped and squelched around in their furry nappies.

42

The Unbearable Heaviness of Stephen Seagull.

They went back to the cabin, and Putin slapped two glasses down hard onto the table and filled them to the brim with the vodka.

"Here's to real men Stephen" he said, raising his glass in a toast.

"To real men".

"You have enjoyed your time with me Stephen, and I have enjoyed it too. I feel that we will be friends for life, and enjoy many a wrestle together in the future. With my influence and your great films I feel that we can turn this wet, liberal tide that is infecting our men around and make them strong again! Will you join me in this quest?"

"Yes, Vladimir, yes I will".

Putin grinned a massive grin and pulled his chair around until it was right next to Getting-A-Bit-Chunky-There-Stevie's chair, their furry nappies touching and their oily thighs rubbing against each other.

"I knew you wouldn't let me down Stephen, now, let us seal this deal with a long, lingering and manly cuddle".

The Unbearable Heaviness of Stephen Seagull.

Getting-A-Bit-Chunky-There-Stevie spent the best part of six months in Russia, and felt really refreshed and not at all sexually confused by the end of it. He had made a friend for life in Putin, and promised that they would regularly swap photos of both of them practising their martial arts moves in their pants (for reasons he couldn't quite remember). He had formed a real love of Russia and its people, but despite this he felt that it was time to return home, and resume his film career with vigour anew.

As soon as he got home and packed away his furry nappies etc. he popped to the laundrette to see his agent, hoping for some good news about his career.

"Stephen, great to see you!" His agent beamed, stuffing some clean slacks into a bin bag. "How was your break?"

"It was wonderful thanks Hector, just what the doctor ordered. Anyway, down to business, have you had any offers for me?"

"I have actually, believe it or not! Come into my office". They entered the men's toilet, and Hector pulled a carrier bag down from the top of the cistern. "Let's have a look...well there's an offer here from a Mexican soap, a six-month contract playing a gone-to-seed hitman doing small assassinations to pay for his diabetes and gout treatment; apparently it was written specifically with you in mind. No? Okay, well there's this one here then, a part in an action ensemble film Killed Again. They want you to play the baddie, a drug-dealing paedophile who likes to put live penguins and kittens into a blender while interrogating his enemies, all while he plays the Grease soundtrack at ear-splitting volume.

"No no no no no, there is NO way my fans would ever respect me again in a film after playing a character that awful; there is not a chance in HELL I will ever play a Bee Gees fan".

"Okay fine, there is one more part, a lead role in a film for a small independent company, where you play a former special forces ace now living a quiet life working in a call centre for a mobile phone company. One day you discover that the pretty young girl who sits opposite you is being blackmailed into posing for pornographic pictures by the local mafia, and you are forced to come out of fighting retirement to kick muthafuckin' ass".

"At last, finally you offer me something I can get my teeth into. That sounds like a fresh, novel idea that I could really do something with, so set up a meeting will you?"

"Great Stephen! I'll get on the phone to them pronto, or at least as soon as I've got this stubborn and unidentifiable stain out of these underpants".

The Unbearable Heaviness of Stephen Seagull.

Two weeks later Getting-A-Bit-Chunky-There-Stevie was waiting in a disused public toilet which had been made up to look like a call centre, ready to begin filming. He was quietly confident that playing Laazlo Magnesium would get him right back on top, or at the very least get his foot back on the ladder. Taste These Knuckles Hombre was being directed by Hamilton Smith, who had recently directed a very well-received Anusol advert for Chilean television. Jessica Goodman, a former child actress now trying to make it as a serious adult thespian, was playing the young woman. Deric Roberts was playing the mafia Don, with his main muscle being played by an MMA star that Getting-A-Bit-Chunky-There-Stevie couldn't be arsed learning the name of. Getting-A-Bit-Chunky-There-Stevie was once again providing the soundtrack, and was loosening up his fingers doodling around on the old Bontempi when Jessica entered the building, gagging slightly at the pishy smell that still lingered in these former bogs.

"Hello Stephen, I'm looking forward to working with you" she said, smiling and holding out an outstretched hand.

I bet you are you saucy minx, he thought to himself. She was twenty-two and he was forty- nine, but he was willing to overlook the age difference and pork her, as she so clearly wanted.

"Nice to meet you too Jessica, I loved your work in that film of yours I watched, honestly. Are you looking forward to the love scene between our characters?"

"What? I can't remember there being a love scene in the script".

"One of the main actors in this did a bit of script-doctoring recently as per his demands, and a love scene was inserted between our characters. I happened to see that your contract has no mention of a no nudity clause".

"When did you see my contract? I thought they were private? And I don't wish to do nudity thank you if that's what you're suggesting; I'll have to have a word with the director and clear some things up".

"I um…didn't actually demand to see your contract, I was just assuming that was the case. I think you'll find though that the contract you signed does say that you have to honour any script changes that may occur during filming".

"I can't recall seeing anything in my contract about that".

"No, it's definitely in there, on the back of the page. In tiny writing. In Urdu. But it IS there. Anyway, I was thinking that while you are straddling me in the scene, perhaps it would look more emotional and realistic if instead of sitting on my belly as is usual in these kind of scenes, you sat a little bit further south".

"Sorry Stephen, I REALLY need to go and talk to the director". She stormed out of the bogs, and Getting-A-Bit-Chunky-There-Stevie shrugged and resumed eating his pastie.

A little while after this Deric Roberts and the MMA bloke entered, MMA bloke eyeing Getting-A-Bit-Chunky-There-Stevie with just a hint of distain.

"Hi Stephen, great to see you again" Deric said.

The Unbearable Heaviness of Stephen Seagull.

"Oh, have we met?"

"Stephen! How could you! Don't you remember? We filmed Panzer Party for three months in Belgravia together, I played your brother".

"Oh…yeah…I remember…sorry, I didn't recognise you with that different t-shirt on."

"We also did Alligator Kronktite and His Band of Bastards 1, 2, 3 and 4 together too, as well as Are You Talking to Me Or Chewing A Brick?, Chaffinch Squadron, I'll Break Your Cankles, and Machine-Face. Oh, and we also did that two-year run filming the Doomwatcher TV series together, in which we were the main adversaries and you ended up killing me with my own dachshund".

"Yes, yes, I've said that I remember you Alec".

"Deric".

"Yes, Deric".

"This here is Madddissson MacNulty, one of the toughest men you are ever likely to meet. He isn't just an actor, a pretend tough-guy like us, he's the real deal".

Madddissson said nothing, and just stood there looking at Getting-A-Bit-Chunky-There-Stevie with his arms folded.

"I think you will find that I AM a legitimate tough guy Ale…Deric" Getting-A-Bit-Chunky-There-Stevie said angrily. "I could teach this young whippersnapper a thing or two, that's for sure. I was killing spies undercover in Botswana and Eritrea back when he was at his mother's tit".

Madddissson snorted derisively, but said nothing.

"You gotta problem with what I said, mute-boy?"

"I'd eat you for breakfast old man" Madddissson said, staring coldly at Getting-A-Bit-Chunky-There-Stevie. "Though you'd probably LITERALLY try and eat me for breakfast by the look of you".

Getting-A-Bit-Chunky-There-Stevie heaved himself up from his seat with a grunt, and squared up to Madddissson. Well, rounded up to him.

"You remind me of a bitch-ass punk who tried it on with me in Chechnya, except that he was about a foot taller than you are. After I was finished with him he looked like something you'd find lying on the floor of an abattoir, and I'd be happy to do the same to you, little man".

"Woah woah guys" Deric said, intervening, "let's just calm down, okay? We're going to be working together for the next few weeks, so let's just try and get along eh?"

"Just keep him out of my face" Getting-A-Bit-Chunky-There-Stevie said, sitting back down to his crisps, trying to disguise the fact he was a bit dizzy after standing up too fast.

"That's gonna be pretty hard for me" said Madddissson, grinning. "It's that big I couldn't keep out of its way even if I tried".

46

The Unbearable Heaviness of Stephen Seagull.

Getting-A-bit-Chunky-There-Stevie tried to get up again but didn't quite manage, and sat back down again, dizzy.

"Come on Madddissson, I think it's time you left" Deric said, leading the MMA star away. "It was nice to meet you again Stephen, and I look forward to working with you again".

"Bye Alec".

Half an hour later they were filming the first scene of the film, in which Laazlo was dealing with a stroppy customer on the other end of the line at work when he notices Samantha, the young woman, is crying. His caring, though tough as fuck character immediately hangs up on the wittering idiot on the other end of the line and walks over to her, laying a comforting hand on her shoulder. Jessica flinched slightly, which wasn't in the script, but hopefully they could edit that out (the budget meant that they couldn't afford more than one take per scene), and looked up at Laazlo.

"What's wrong pretty lady?"

"Oh I wouldn't want to worry a handsome man like you, I'll be okay".

Laazlo sat down on the conveniently empty chair next to her, disguising his grunt with a cough.

"No, I can clearly see that you are not okay, you can tell me".

"Some men are forcing me to do some things I'm not into but I really don't know how to get out of it, my life is such a mess".

"Ah, I see, and you don't have a man to sort everything out for you I take it?"

"No, I've been single for over a year now, and without any masculine guidance my life has fallen to pieces; understandably".

"What kind of things are we talking about here?"

"They're making me do pornographic pictures, like these ones".

She held up five photographs of herself in a variety of compromising positions, showing him in such a way that the camera got a good lingering look as well. "Now they are talking about moving me into films next; oh Laazlo, I don't know what to do!"

Laazlo put a comforting arm around her back, and kissed her on the head. Jessica flinched slightly again, annoyingly, but he was confident this action was hidden from the camera by his bulk.

"Don't you worry your sweet little empty head about this any longer, I know someone who will take care of these horrible men".

She looked up, a faint flicker of hope etched across her weeping face.

"Really, who?"

He chuckled wryly, and ruffled her hair.

The Unbearable Heaviness of Stephen Seagull.

"Probably the toughest call centre worker in all the land, but I can't name names". He winked at her, and walked back to his chair.

End of scene.

"That was great people, just great!" Hamilton enthused with a small clap. "Let's break for lunch while the stuntmen set up the next scene.

Getting-A-Bit-Chunky-There-Stevie had inserted a clause into his contract stipulating that there had to be four lunches per day, and he was looking forward to the sausage, liver and onion baps spread out on the table before him. He had a really good feeling about the film, and felt that the fact that some of the clothing was made out of paper due to budgetary constraints wasn't really important, and probably wouldn't look as crap onscreen (and they'd probably be able to edit out the rustling in post-production). His fee wasn't brilliant, but with the sausage roll-related clauses and the fact that he was going to be allowed to take any clothing his character wore home after filming was finished, it was still going to end up being a profitable time for him (though of course he wouldn't be able to wear most of the newly-acquired attire in the rain).

A slight fly in the ointment was that Jessica had tried to get out of her contract, after discovering that Getting-A-Bit-Chunky-There-Stevie had been allowed to extensively re-write the script, her argument being that the pornographic photography scenes could easily be implied rather than explicitly shown so many, many times. However Stephen was adamant that the audience NEEDED to see her suffering in all of its raw, painful, degrading and sexy detail. Thankfully, her contract was water-tight and she couldn't get out of it, but it did make the atmosphere on set rather strained. This wasn't helped by Madddissson regularly taunting Getting-A-Bit-Chunky-There-Stevie, and trying to goad him into a physical confrontation. Many times Deric had to jump between the two alpha males, and defuse the situation with a sausage roll or two.

Things finally came to a head during one of the final fight scenes, where the two men had to square off against each other, with Laazlo eventually winning in style. During filming of the scene Madddissson seemed to have other ideas, and kept getting the better of Getting-A-Bit-Chunky-There-Stevie, though of course Getting-A-Bit-Chunky-There-Stevie was holding back. After fifteen minutes of this a sweaty Getting-A-Bit-Chunky-There-Stevie was livid, and shoved Madddissson angrily away.

"Calm the fuck down boy!" He yelled, face crimson (partly in anger, partly in exertion) "or shit gets real!"

"Ha! I WANT shit to get real! Any time you wanna go, let's go!"

Getting-A-Bit-Chunky-There-Stevie advanced, fists clenched, and eyeballed him from about a foot away.

"Bring it on pussy, I ate guys like you for breakfast when I was undercover in Singapore".

He got into a fighting stance, but then he suddenly remembered that Deric had taken the day off work to cut a friend's grass, cash-in-hand, and a fear-fart squeaked out of his arse. His eyes darted to the director, but Hamilton was busy chatting up an extra, and wasn't even noticing the commotion.

"I said, BRING IT ON PUSSY!" he yelled as loud as he could, but when he glanced at Hamilton he was still enraptured by an ample cleavage, and probably wouldn't notice a nuclear bomb going off.

48

The Unbearable Heaviness of Stephen Seagull.

Madddissson stripped off his top, to reveal a rippling, athletic and powerful torso. Getting-A-Bit-Chunky-There-Stevie decided that he would keep his top on. He threw a sneaky punch at Madddissson's face, but the MMA star easily evaded it, and chuckled.

"Oh my god you are priceless! What the hell was that!"

"I was just getting my range" Getting-A-Bit-Chunky-There-Stevie replied, slightly out of breath.

"Oh okay, have you got it now then? Fancy another go?"

Getting-A-Bit-Chunky-There-Stevie threw another punch, which Madddissson also dodged, and compounded this with throwing a playful little slap at Getting-A-Bit-Chunky-There-Stevie's cheek. Getting-A-Bit-Chunky-There-Stevie tried a different approach and sent out a kick towards Madddissson's knee, but felt a sudden twang in his arse cheek, and winced in pain. As he rubbed his throbbing arse-cheek and stood there sweating and panting, Madddissson swiftly pulled Getting-A-Bit-Chunky-There-Stevie's t-shirt up and began slapping his belly, then reached behind and gave him a wedgie.

As Getting-A-Bit-Chunky-There-Stevie flapped around trying to sort his undies out Madddissson just stood there, cracking up with laughter.

"I knew it! I knew you were all talk, you wheezing piece of shit! Oh I am going to have so much fun kicking your ass!"

He grabbed a flailing Getting-A-Bit-Chunky-There-Stevie around the waist and, squeezing hard, headbutted him twice on the nose, breaking it. Unfortunately for him the previous few hours sausage rolls, cans of cola, crisps, ice cream, bacon rolls and Mars Bars had resulted in a potent stew of gasses brewing in Getting-A-Bit-Chunky-There-Stevie's expansive belly, and as Madddissson squeezed he forced a massive, loud, and rumbling fart to explode out of Getting-A-Bit-Chunky-There-Stevie's anus, along with a tiny little bit of its more solid cousin. As the smell hit his nostrils he instantly let go of his chunky foe, and started coughing and gagging.

"Oh...my...god...what...the hell..."he spluttered, doubled over, retching. Getting-A-Bit-Chunky-There-Stevie saw his chance, and, wincing with the pain from his nose, grabbed a fire extinguisher from the wall and battered Madddissson over the head with it twice, knocking him to the ground. Madddissson struggled onto his hands and knees, blood gushing from a deep wound in his head. Getting-A-Bit-Chunky-There-Stevie seized the opportunity and kicked him hard in the face, then followed it up with some more kicks to the ribs, causing Madddissson to curl up into a ball. Making sure that no-one was looking, Getting-A-Bit-Chunky-There-Stevie grabbed the extinguisher again and hit Madddissson a few more times around the body with it, until his opponent muttered weakly that he'd had enough. Getting-A-Bit-Chunky-There-Stevie quickly put the extinguisher back on the wall and flopped down into his seat, gasping for air.

A few minutes later a stuntman walked into the room and stopped with a surprised look on his face, looking at Madddissson, still prone on the ground, and Getting-A-Bit-Chunky-There-Stevie sitting in the chair, his breath finally back and smiling cockily.

"What happened?" the stuntman asked, the shocked look still on his face.
49

The Unbearable Heaviness of Stephen Seagull.

"A young rival challenged the reigning alpha of the pack and soon regretted the decision" Getting-A-Bit-Chunky-There-Stevie replied, as he coolly opened a packet of cheesy Wotsits.

"Is he okay? And what the holy hell is that smell? My god, it's like a hippo shat out a sewage plant".

Getting-A-Bit-Chunky-There-Stevie chuckled wryly, and smiled a Wotsit-speckled smile.

"I think the poor wannabe on the floor soiled himself in fear, when he realised just how out of his depth he was".

"Have you been crying?"

"What? No, don't be ridiculous, as if the throbbing, unending pain of a broken nose would cause ME to cry; my eyes are watering with the stench coming from captain Scaredy-cat down there, that's all". He got up from the chair with a grunt, licking Wotsit residue from his fingers. "I'm going to my trailer for a nap, wake me when the buffet is open".

He walked away, bowing his head in case he met anyone on the way to his trailer and they saw the fresh batch of tears that had begun to leak from his eyes. At that point, he really wanted his mummy.

The Unbearable Heaviness of Stephen Seagull.

Madddissson ended up getting fired from the film due to him attacking the "star", and despite his protestations as to how the fight actually went most believed this to be simply sour grapes from the loser, and Getting-A-Bit-Chunky-There-Stevie kept his title as the toughest man in Hollywood.

Named Stephen.

With a ponytail.

And type two diabetes.

Despite decent reviews though ("you can barely hear the rustling of the suits in some scenes"- The Berkshire Nitwit; "Realistic call-centre operations"- Call Centre Monthly; "some decent fight scenes, and the large gentlemen wasn't TOO sweaty in some of them"- The Berlin Star), the film underperformed at the box office yet again, which angered Getting-A-Bit-Chunky-There-Stevie, who laid the blame squarely at the feet of the film company. He decided that the time had come to dispense with film companies altogether and deal with everything himself from now on, by forming his own company. Punchy Ponytail Productions would show them all how to do this thing properly, and from now on he wouldn't have to answer to anyone.

Initially the bank wasn't too keen to loan him any money for the new business, but a quick phone call (plus some photos of himself fighting in his pants) to Putin resulted in some Russian heavies coming over and "persuading" the manager of the bank otherwise, and now our hero had some serious cash to invest in his first film for the exciting new company: The Fightin' Irish(man, who is actually from America). In it Getting-A-Bit-Chunky-There-Stevie would be playing Sam Begorrah, an American who becomes a world champion kickboxing star despite his "advanced" years and girth. He is asked to throw a world championship fight by the Russian mafia and their boss, Englishman Cockney Fred (played by Nicholas Cage, doing his usual shite). He also has a daughter in a wheelchair who needs an urgent life-saving operation, and the money the mafia are offering him will pay for this, and then some. Sam has to wrestle with saving his daughter or upholding professional sport's pure moral code, and all while trying to pump his promoter Jill Hassenpfeffer (Nicholas Cage again in drag, to prove he can be shite in a variety of roles).

The film doesn't do great business at the box-office, but due to its small budget, Cage accepting one fee for two parts, and Getting-A-Bit-Chunky-There-Stevie managing to sell on the film to various TV companies to show late at night on a Thursday, it actually managed to turn a small profit, which Getting-A-Bit-Chunky-There-Stevie invested straight into his next project: Killer Cockerel. This film was equally (minorly) successful, and Getting-A-Bit-Chunky-There-Stevie realised that he was onto a winning formula, something he tweaked further by deciding to forego the hassle of releasing the film into the cinema, and instead deciding to go straight to DVD, which he saw as the future; cinema was on its way out, in his eyes.

The Unbearable Heaviness of Stephen Seagull.

Many years passed, and Big Stevie and his company had amassed quite a portfolio of films, with the occasional one even being not-entirely-pish. He was now renting a lovely, compact bungalow a mere three hours drive in his rented car from his company's base on the outskirts of Hollywood, and he was once or twice a year flying over to Russia to give demonstrations on fighting to gullib...fresh-faced students, and meet up with his old pal Putin. Life was good, and apart from perhaps having a bit more money, glass in the windows of his home, relief from his gout, his young Russian bride speaking English and not puling THOSE faces when he motioned going to the bedroom, and missing some of the possessions he'd had to sell to keep the company afloat, he couldn't ask for more. As he pulled on his rented socks and rented shoes and walked out into the sunshine to head into work to begin filming Ya wanna Piece of Me Cancer?, a small smile crossed his lips, as he thought about how far he had come from that little boy all those years ago, sitting at home watching martial arts films while his parents entertained the local football team upstairs.

He had released a couple of blues albums with his band, and had decided that the sales didn't matter; all the coolest bluesmen had not been appreciated until after their deaths, and he was confident that the same would be the case with his music. All in all life was good, and if they would only develop a cheeseburger flavoured ice cream then it might even become a little bit great.

An offer had come in to star in a film with rising action star Brogan Mannigan, a rare opportunity to co-star in a Hollywood production that would be released into cinema. Big Stevie honestly didn't care that none of his films had been released to cinema for many, many years, didn't care one little bit, no siree, no way, but it might be nice just for old time's sake to be in a film that had an international release into the cinema again. He was to star as Maxton Hegrinator, a former mafia hitman who had managed to escape from his criminal past and had reinvented himself as a driving instructor in a small rural village, where he was a member of the local amateur dramatic society and keen florist. Brogan Mannigan was to be a former colleague in the mafia who accidently discovers where Maxton is now living a quiet life, and vows to make him pay for leaving the organisation without permission. Big Stevie's fee was going to be bigger than he had earned in quite a while, and would enable him to buy his own toaster and cutlery, and get his underwear back from the pawn shop. As soon as he had finished filming Ya Wanna Piece of me Cancer? He was to fly straight to New York to begin filming this exciting Hollywood project, and he was looking forward to doing a film where he could just concentrate on acting, without having to worry about all the other business interests involved in running your own, um, "thriving" film company.

The Unbearable Heaviness of Stephen Seagull.

Ah, New York, New York, so good they named it, he thought to himself as he stepped off the plane. It was good to be back in the city where so many of his classic films had been made: Rock Fist; Mr. Bicep; Rock, Scissor, Bazooka; Warrior of the Igloo; Fights Like the Wind; Navajo Mercenary; The Six-Shooter Six-Footer, and many more. He was being met by the producer who was apparently a big fan, and who would drive him to the hotel that would be his home for the next nine or so weeks of filming.

"Hello Stephen".

Big Stevie approached the portly little gentleman standing holding the "STEPHEN SEAGULL" cardboard sign, and shook his hand.

"Hello Mr. Formica, it's great to back in such a wonderful city".

"Glad you like it Stephen. Now I'm sure you're hungry, so let's go to my car and we can go and get something to eat and drink; I'm sure it's been a tiring flight for you".

"Yes, plane seats seem to be made incredibly small nowadays, I couldn't wait to land to be honest".

They walked out to the car and made their way to the hotel, stopping off on the way at a small diner. Big Stevie unpacked, showered, wanked, showered again, had a few snacks from the fridge in the room, and then dressed and walked down to the front of the hotel, where Mr. Formica had said he would pick Big Stevie up in two hours. This he did on the dot, and the pair of them drove to the studio to meet the rest of the cast and crew for a welcoming party.

"Stephen, this is Brogan Mannigan, your co-star in Rural Rampage".

Big Stevie managed to hide his sneer as he set eyes upon the latest pretender to his throne. He could see that here was yet another chancer who mistook being in his physical prime, tall, muscular and an expert in martial arts, with being tough and able to handle yourself in a fight. Big Stevie could make him cry with a flick of his index finger, and he was confident that this latest wannabe could sense this too, deep down.

"Hello Brogan, nice to meet you".

"Hi Stephen, I'm a big fan of yours, Cranial Breakage inspired me to get into acting as a young teen".

"Well Brogan, I've heard good things about you too (this was a lie of course, Big Stevie couldn't give less of a shit about his inferior "rivals" and never paid any attention to their careers). I've noticed that in one scene in this film your character manages to overpower me and take me captive, I presume that you sneak up on me or something? I can't imagine that my fans would find this very realistic otherwise".

Brogan exchanged a glance with Mr. Formica.

"Your character wins at the end of the film Stephen, so I don't think it really matters if you lose a battle but win the war eh? It makes the film more exciting, so people don't know that the result is a foregone conclusion".

"Hmmmn, I beg to differ, but no matter. Anyway, I look forward to our scenes together, and I'm sure that you will learn quite a lot from the experience".

The Unbearable Heaviness of Stephen Seagull.

"Yes...I'm sure I will Stephen. Sorry, but I'm being beckoned over to the far corner of the room, nice to have met you".

He departed, and Mr. Formica led Big Stevie over to a young woman near the buffet. Big Stevie felt an instant attraction, and could feel a semi rising in his trousers as he stared in awe at the vision of perfection in front of him: egg and cress sandwiches, cakes, sausage rolls, pizza slices, a selection of cheeses, a selection of dips, and some other stuff obscured by the bint standing in front of the table.

"Stephen, this is Jane Addison, another of your co-stars in the film".

"Oh yeah, hi" Big Stevie replied, trying to see past her.

"Jane will be playing the third main character in the film, Gertrude Bartholomew".

"So, my love interest I take it" Big Stevie said, giving her body a quick scan for a rating: eight out of ten, needs to show more cleavage.

"Actually, I play the head of police in the village, who is also head of the horticultural society in her free time".

Big Stevie couldn't help a little chuckle escaping his lips.

"Will people really buy that, a woman in charge of a police station?"

"What era of prehistory did they dig this fossil up from?" Jane asked Mr. Formica. "For your information women are now in positions of power and able to drive and everything!"

Big Stevie looked bemused, and made a "what's she like" roll of his eyes to Mr. Formica.

"I hate to burst your bubble Stephen" she continued, irately. "But if you have a look at the script then you'll find that my character actually has more lines than your one does".

"My characters are always the strong, silent type anyway, so that doesn't bother me at all. Anyway you didn't answer the question, will you be my love interest in the film?"

"No Stephen" she replied in an exasperated tone "I don't play anyone's love interest in the film; I am the head of police who uncovers the reasons behind Brogan's character coming to the village and that is IT! Well, apart from judging the best floral display section of the village fete".

"Lesbian then? I suppose that would explain why she enters such a masculine profession, and manages to pass through the ranks to such a high position of power"". He turned to Mr. Formica. "I suppose we could have her character question her sexuality when she meets my character, and fall in love with me at the floral awards".

Jane shot him a look and stormed off, leaving Big Stevie a perfect view of the buffet at last.

"Tch, typical lesbian" he muttered to Mr. Formica, as he picked up a plate. Mr. Formica explained to Big Stevie that he had to go to the toilet for a long time, and left the room. Big Stevie looked around at the other occupants of the room, and sighed. It looked like he was going to have to provide the necessary charisma in this film yet again. There wasn't one of these large, fit young men who could realistically

The Unbearable Heaviness of Stephen Seagull.

beat him up whether on film or in real life, and there seemed to be an awful lot of women in the room for an action film. Still, he would bless the party with his presence for another few hours, not least because few of them seemed to be touching the buffet with any degree of relish, so that was more for him.

The Unbearable Heaviness of Stephen Seagull.

Week three of filming on Rural Rampage was going okay, though Big Stevie was still trying to pressure the director to provide a female admirer or seven for his character, to make it more realistic. He was having a break with some of the crew while the set was being altered for the next scene. A couple of the crew were having a bit of a wrestle around in the car park, and a small crowd had gathered to watch their horseplay. Big Stevie walked over, eager to hand out some fighting tips to these clueless beginners in the art of warfare.

"Jack Wins!" a stuntman acting as referee shouted, holding up Jack's hand in triumph. His opponent pretended to be livid at the outcome, to laughter from the crowd.

"Jack White remains the undefeated champion of backstage wrestling" the referee continued, though of course thls is only because Gene repeatedly declines to enter the competition". The crowd laughed some more, and an elderly gentlemen held up his hands and waved humbly to the crowd.

Big Stevie walked into the centre of the car park, and eyed the two wrestlers.

"So you think you can wrestle eh?" he asked, looking around at the crowd with a smile on his piggy face. "I wouldn't exactly call what I just witnessed wrestling, more like two little girls practising their kissing techniques".

"Ah come on Stephen, it's just a bit of fun between takes" A voice called from the crowd "it's not the world championships".

Big Stevie turned his eyes to the speaker, the smile falling from his face. "Fighting is NEVER just a bit of fun, but only real warriors understand this".

"Chill out Stephen" an extra in the crowd said, amongst muttering from the rest of the onlookers. "it's just a bit of a laugh".

"It wasn't a laugh when I had to fight off fourteen warriors to save my platoon when fighting in Kosovo, it wasn't a laugh when killing six enemy special forces commandos when breaking up a siege in Botswana, and it wasn't a laugh when I downed an enemy helicopter with nothing more than a penny whistle back in 'Nam. People like me don't fight for a laugh, we fight to the death, something soft layabouts on a film set will never understand. If any of you tried any of your wrestling shit on me you would be waking up in the morning with every limb broken".

"I've heard Madddissson kicked your ass on set years ago" a voice cried from the back, causing a ripple of laughter to emanate from the rest of the crowd.

"Who said that?" Big Stevie spat, scanning the crowd for the culprit.

"Come on Stephen" the referee said, "you're an actor, not a soldier".

Big Stevie approached him angrily. "I could beat every single person on this set with one hand tied behind my back and the other eating a sandwich; no-one on this planet could beat me, NO-ONE!"

He squared up to the ref threateningly.

The Unbearable Heaviness of Stephen Seagull.

"Okay Stephen, just calm down there big fella" a voice from behind said soothingly. Big Stevie turned around and saw it was the elderly man from earlier.

"Who the fuck are you?" Big Stevie asked, eyeballing him furiously.

"My name is Gene LuvsJezebelle" the man said, extending a welcoming hand, which Big Stevie chose to ignore. "I'm a stuntman on this film, as well as a martial arts veteran of some years standing. These men are just blowing off some steam backstage Stephen, no harm done".

Big Stevie continued to eyeball him. "I don't care, I dislike seeing weak little nobodies like this making out that fighting is easy, and anyone can do it. I'm known as one of the toughest men on the planet, definitely in the top two, and I don't like to see the warrior lifestyle played for laughs and fun; it's a serious business, where people die, usually at my hands".

Gene smiled. "On film, yes".

"No, in real life when they dare to awaken the beast. No-one in Hollywood is even playing the same game as me, never mind belongs in the same league".

"Okay Stephen, tell you what, how about we have a little spar right here? Just a little workout?"

Big Stevie snorted. "With you? I don't think so. I don't fight old men, I wouldn't want your death on my conscience".

"Come on Stephen, if I feel faint or anything I'll tap out, you have my word".

"Well okay then old man, it's your funeral, let's go".

He crouched into a fighting stance, and then everything went black.

"Wh..what happened? Did I kill him?"

Big Stevie was confused, and looked up at the faces looking down at him in puzzlement. He couldn't figure out why they seemed so much taller than him, until he eventually came to understand that he was lying down. He became vaguely aware that his bottom half felt very warm, and became worried that he was covered in the blood of the old man. He sat up groggily, aware of laughter in the background.

"Is...is the old man okay?" he asked, as he stumbled up onto his feet, dimly aware of more thick blood running down the back of his trousers.

"Oh Gene's perfectly fine Stephen" a woman said to him, gagging slightly.

"You never touched him Stephen" another woman said, giggling. "He's away filming his next stunt".

"I don't understand" Big Stevie said, noticing a vile smell coming from somewhere nearby.

"Gene choked you out and you fell instantly Stephen".

"Huh? That can't be right, he must have sucker-punched me or something. Did he have an accomplice?"

The Unbearable Heaviness of Stephen Seagull.

"No, it was just him Stephen", a man from the crowd said, walking towards Big Stevie with a mixture of amusement and revulsion on his face. "Now I think you'd better maybe go to your trailer and get cleaned up before your next scene".

He gently took Big Stevie by the arm and led him through the crowd, who parted with that same mixture of amusement and revulsion on their faces.

As Big Stevie walked he could feel a warmth running down his legs and squelching in between his toes and he finally understood just how sick and ungentlemanly this Gene character had been. Not only had he obviously made use of at least one accomplice (no matter what that man in the crowd, who may even have been one of them, had said), but when the accomplice(s) had somehow managed to sneak up on Big Stevie and with great effort managed to temporarily knock him out, this sick Gene bastard had shown his utter lack of the noble code that TRUE warriors lived by, and must have pulled down Big Stevie's trousers and shat down his legs.

The Unbearable Heaviness of Stephen Seagull.

The filming of Rural Rampage passed without further incident and opened to relatively decent reviews ("the judging in the floral awards seemed a bit amiss, as Mrs. Higginbottom had a clearly superior display, but other than that the film fulfilled all of the criteria necessary to be called an action film"-The Peru Film and Snorkelling Review; "Yeah, middling. Now, does anyone know where I can hire a combine harvester?"-Sussex Angler Magazine; "Stephen Seagull fills the screen with his presence"-The Inverness Chronicle), and for a brief moment Big Stevie thought that Hollywood might have opened up again to him, but unfortunately no more offers were forthcoming, and he soon retreated back to his own film company. Not that this mattered at all, I mean, who needs Hollywood anyway? Not Big Stevie, not on your or anyone else's Nelly. For the rest of his career nasty rumours about what had happened in the fight with the old stuntman would dog him, but he knew that this was just jealousy rearing its ugly head, and people who wouldn't dare to challenge him in a physical confrontation trying to belittle him behind his back to make themselves look better.

Over the next few years he would continue to produce quality films at an astonishing rate, and though the likes of Demon Kill, Chinese Burn, Kill on Kommand, Atishoo, Atishoo They All Fall Down, and Meltdown Imminent didn't trouble the awards committees of the art world, most of them turned a profit running well into three figures. Big Stevie consoled himself with the thought that he was simply ahead of his time, and would be hailed as a genius once he had died of obesity-related illness.

Big Stevie decided to give something back, and so he joined the police force. At first he thought about going in straight at the top, but after a little while thinking about it he decided to enter the force at the bottom. His first shift was a time of great excitement for him, and he couldn't wait to kick some criminal ass.

The first shift involved driving around town with his partner Sam "Sam" Jones. Big Stevie was sitting in the passenger seat on that first night, when they got his very first call. There was a disturbance on a street corner which was the haunt of various drug dealers, pimps, and prostitutes, and Big Stevie and Sam were told to go and see what the score was. Big Stevie hoped that his gout and sciatica wouldn't slow him down should there be any trouble (his lumbago had abated recently, so that should be fine).

They pulled up under the streetlights to see ten or twelve people arguing and shoving around across the street. Sam helped Big Stevie out of the car, and the pair of them crossed over to the commotion.

"Hello everyone, is there a problem here?" Sam asked in a friendly tone.

"This muthafucka stole my dru...sweets, and I'm really hungry", a tall, skinny man shouted angrily, pointing accusingly at a shorter stocky bloke.

"Fuck you bitch, I didn't steal shit!"

They started jostling each other around again, as their friends joined in and began threatening and shoving each other around.

"Okay okay, let's just calm down people" Sam shouted, getting in between the main two. "I'm sure we can settle this amicably, so let's just stop the shouting and pushing around and we can all go home to our own beds tonight".

The Unbearable Heaviness of Stephen Seagull.

"Fuck that! This bitch is getting it!" The stocky guy pulled back his fist and squared up to the taller one, but was held back by a hand on his shoulder. He turned around to see Big Stevie standing there, shaking his head.

"I wouldn't do that if I were you" Big Stevie said, ponytail glistening in the streetlights. "Now let's shake hands like good little boys, and daddy won't get angry with you".

"Are you threating us muthafucka? Are you really a policeman? You look familiar".

Big Stevie chuckled.

"I would imagine that I DO look familiar...You'll have seen Chimpanzee Cage Rage?"

Everyone standing around looked at each other, and shook their heads, with a few answering in the negative.

"Okay, well I suppose that film WAS a while ago, what about The Karate Preacher?"

More headshakes and murmurs of "no" from the crowd.

"Bullet in the Face?"

Ditto.

"Cro-Magnon Hitman?"

"The Beast from the Mid-South-East?"

"Iron Knuckle?"

"Shaolin Monkey Butler?"

"Cracking Craniums?"

"Crank McAllister and the Scorpions of Death? Do you people not have a cinema around here?"

"Master of Mayhem?"

(Forty-three minutes later).

"Medieval Kickass?"

"Cemetery Filler?"

"Platoon Squadron?"

"Gun Beats Sword?"

"Trapped on a Big Ship?"

"Yes! Yes! I know that one!" a voice called from the section of the crowd who were still awake and hadn't wandered off. "My dad had it on VHS! I used to watch it in my teens".

A few others joined in, saying that they too remembered Trapped on a Big Ship.

The Unbearable Heaviness of Stephen Seagull.

"At last, finally you knuckleheads have shown a modicum of good taste; I was beginning to worry about the younger generation's education for a moment there" Big Stevie said, exasperated.

"Anyway, what about the film?"

"I was in it!" Big Stevie shouted angrily "that's what this whole discussion has been about!"

"Ah...right. Oh, I see, you're saying THAT'S why I find you familiar! I forgot why this all started".

"Can I go home now?" One of the crowd asked, bored.

The rest of the crowd looked at Big Stevie with hope. He sighed, and waved them away.

"Yeah yeah, all of you just go home, and maybe watch a film or two before you come back out again. Philistines".

The crowd dispersed in separate directions, and Big Stevie gently woke up the ones sleeping on the pavement. Sam came walking over, having buggered off for a coffee about twenty minutes ago.

"Everything sorted out now Stephen?" He asked, handing Big Stevie a coffee.

"Yes, I put a stop to their violence with my alpha-male dominance".

Sam smiled "You're a natural at this Stephen, maybe you've finally found your calling".

"Well actually I think you will find that I've added to all of my other callings: actor; musician; scriptwriter; special forces op; bodyguard; door security; composer; company director; producer; stuntman; martial arts trainer; philosopher; chef; taxi driver; fireman; pilot; presidential aide; astronaut; palaeontologist; medic; motorcycle courier; sniper; Arthurian knight; Mongol warrior; jungle guide..."

"Aren't many of those things just parts you've played in your films?" Sam interrupted, wanting to get home at some point that night.

"You honestly think that my films are purely fiction? Do you never wonder why when I've played all these parts that the characters look EXACTLY like the real life me? It's hardly going to be coincidence, is it?"

"Well I can't argue with that impeccable logic" Sam said wearily, heading back to the patrol car.

"Didn't you get any doughnuts?" Big Stevie asked, following him.

They got into the car and drove around town for a while, Big Stevie "regaling" Sam with stories from his special forces days, all while emphasising to Sam that those investigations into his past that the media did a few years ago which said that he made everything up, was complete bollocks rooted in envy. Eventually they got another call to investigate an argument at a house on the outskirts of town. They got to the house and got out of the car, walking to the door and ringing the bell. Inside they could hear arguing between a man and a woman which halted for a moment when the bell was rung. They heard shuffling around inside, and Sam was just about to ring the bell again when a gunshot blasted out, and a dull thud hit the grass just a few feet away. Big Stevie let out a yelp and jumped onto Sam, knocking him to the ground. Big Stevie scrambled behind a small wall, panting with fear. He fearfully glanced towards

The Unbearable Heaviness of Stephen Seagull.

Sam, who was lying on the grass, winded. A man was yelling obscenities from somewhere in the house out into the garden, telling whoever was out there to kindly vacate the premises. Big Stevie thought that this was a really good idea and that couples argue all the time anyway, but Sam seemed to have other ideas.

The twat.

Sam staggered to his feet, clutching his side, and approached the door.

"This is the police! Lay down the weapon and approach the door!" Sam had drawn his own weapon, and Big Stevie cursed him inwardly.

"Stephen! Back me up here!" Sam shouted, turning towards where Stephen was hidi...strategically under cover. Fuck, he thought to himself, and willed his body into motion. He crept towards Sam in a crouch, copious bottom-burps squeezing out in fear as he did so.

"Are you okay Stephen?"

"I...I'm...p...perfectly...f...fine".

"You don't sound fine, maybe you should go and wait in the car; this is real life now, not Hollywood".

"I said I'm p...perfectly fine! I just have a coffee allergy which causes me to stutter, that's all. I've been under fire countless times in my life Sam, this is nothing new for me".

"Yes but these aren't blanks this time Stephen. Just go back to the car, I can handle this myself; you're just a rookie after all".

"We're partners Sam, and I can handle it".

"Okay then, you go round the back and see if you can get in from there, but please, be careful".

The man continued to shout his threats, and another bullet thudded into the grass from a window somewhere above them. Big Stevie jumped again, and darted quickly around the side of the house. He was eager to prove to Sam that he really was a legitimately bad motherfucker, not some Hollywood fantasist, but at the same time he was shitting a brick big enough to build a house for a family of five to live in comfortably. He crept carefully around to the back of the house, hoping that Sam would have sorted everything out by the time he got there. He saw that there was an outside toilet in the back garden and thought about hiding in there until it all blew over (and he did feel a shit brewing, to be fair), but decided against it. He snuck up to the back door, and with a feeling of dread discovered that it wasn't locked. He carefully opened it, waiting for a horror film-style creak to give him away to whoever was inside, and slowly entered inside, heart thumping in his chest even more than normal. He could hear someone shuffling around in the gloom but couldn't quite see anything, and advanced further towards a small sliver of light around an ajar door towards the front of the building. Looking though the gap he saw an overweight, sweaty, and naked man shouting out towards the living room window, which was behind closed curtains. There was no sign of the woman through the small gap in the door, and Big Stevie realised that he was going to have to enter the room. He pulled out his gun and aimed it towards the man, advancing slowly. Glancing around the room in an attempt to locate the woman he

The Unbearable Heaviness of Stephen Seagull.

approached the shouting, naked, sweaty fat man, until suddenly said fat man, sensing Big Stevie's presence (possibly due to the heavy breathing and occasional slipped out fear- fart), leapt up at Big Stevie and knocked the gun from his hand. The pair of them rolled around on the floor, Big Stevie desperately trying to subdue the man in a way that didn't involve touching unwanted parts of his body. He could feel sweaty belly rubbing against the side of his face and grimaced, and tried not to think about the sweaty balls banging about on top of his shirt. With a grunt he managed to shove the man from off the top of him and pinned him to the floor, his mind totally in denial about the fact that he was now sitting right on top of a lovely set of sweaty male genitals.

Suddenly a shot rang out from somewhere upstairs, and Big Stevie realised that it must have been the woman who had been shooting, not sweaty bloke. Big Stevie got out his handcuffs and chained the man to the radiator, before making his way carefully up the stairs. He walked towards the sound of gunfire, and looking in an open bedroom door he saw a woman, also, naked, sweaty, and corpulent, sitting at the window, brandishing a gun and cackling like a witch. He inched his way into the room, unsure exactly how wrestling a naked woman might look in his report the next day.

"Lay down the weapon asshole".

The woman jumped as she felt the cold steel on her naked back, and laid down the gun.

"Now stand up, slowly, and walk out of the room".

She did as requested, and they walked down to the front door.

"Sam! It's me, Stephen, I'm coming out the front door with one of the baddies, don't shoot".

"Okay".

Big Stevie carefully opened the door, and nudged the woman outside. Sam was waiting, gun raised, and Big Stevie motioned to him to go inside the house. They got the two of them, threw a blanket over them, and put them in the car.

Sam looked at Big Stevie with new-found respect.

"Wow Stephen, that was fantastic work! You have the makings of a real cop!"

"Thanks, it took me back to my secret work back in the Lebanon all those years ago".

They drove back to the station, the couple babbling incoherently in the back, obviously out of their faces on drugs. Their babbling became louder and louder, and Big Stevie could see that Sam was getting increasingly irate; he was nearing retirement, and Big Stevie could tell that he was tired after a long shift. As they drove on Sam and Big Stevie repeatedly told their prisoners to simmer down, but this only appeared to have the opposite effect, and Big Stevie could see Sam getting increasingly crimson in the face.

"Will you two just SHUT THE HELL UP!" He eventually screamed, turning around in his seat to face them, spittle flying from his lips.

"Sam! Look out!"

The Unbearable Heaviness of Stephen Seagull.

Sam looked back around but it was too late; the car hit a truck dead on, and span around three or four times before hitting a wall. Big Stevie blacked out for a moment, and when he came to the car was upside down and in someone's garden. Thankfully, THIS time no-one had come along and defecated into his trousers while he was blacked out, but he could feel the blood rushing to his head as he hung there upside down, and his belly flopped over his face, making it hard to see what was going on.

"Are you okay?"

He heard a voice at the window, and managed to move some belly aside with one hand and turned to the window. An old couple in nightwear were standing looking in, concerned looks on their faces.

"Phone for help, please" Big Stevie wheezed, struggling for breath under the blanket of belly. Before he blacked out once again, he managed to see the old woman turn and walk away quickly into her house, her nightgown tucked into her underwear at the back, giving him a lovely view of wrinkly old arse cheeks jiggling away as he drifted away into oblivion.

The Unbearable Heaviness of Stephen Seagull.

Big Stevie woke up in a hospital bed, with a medical staff fussing around him.

"Ah you're awake I see, good" the doctor said, consulting a chart.

"What happened doc?"

"You were in a car accident Stephen, but don't worry, you just have some minor injuries that will soon clear up, though you may have a little bit of pain for a few days, but nothing that a Paracetamol or two won't ease".

"How is Sam doc, is he okay?"

The smile fell slightly from the doctor's face.

"Unfortunately Sam wasn't quite so lucky Stephen, he has a broken arm and three fractured ribs. These will heal over time, but we're more worried about the mental damage that seems to have occurred. Sam is suffering from amnesia, and cannot recall anything that happened over the past few days, though hopefully this will come back to him eventually".

The reality of this hit Big Stevie hard.

"But I need him to back up my story! For once I actually WAS the hero and not just talking bollo...um, yet again I saved the day, and it would just be nice to have someone that was there to confirm this, though of course his health is far more important to me."

"Well as I say we hope his memory will come back, but there is a chance that it may never do so. Now rest up, I'll be back in a little while".

Typical, thought Big Stevie, it will just be my word that I was yet again a living legend and heroically stormed the house containing armed criminals, and though of course 99% of people will believe me, from past experience there will always be a tiny minority of cynics who claim that I'm making everything up to make myself look tough. There was nothing he could do about it for the moment though, he would just have to wait and see, and in the meantime hope for a bed-bath or two from these pretty nurses.

Later that evening the station chief came to see Big Stevie, bringing grapes FFS, (hadn't he heard of chocolate?).

"Hello Stephen, how are you feeling?"

"Oh, I'm bearing up okay chief, under the circumstances. Is there any word on how Sam is doing?"

"Ah you're a good man Stephen, thinking about others while laid up in hospital yourself. Unfortunately the doctor thinks that Sam's recent short-term memories are gone forever, though thankfully everything is else is still fine, he knows who he is etc. He will need a bit of time off work to heal of course, as will you".

Big Stevie really couldn't believe his bad luck...His only hope now would be to make a film based on the night in question, that would let everyone know the truth. He vowed to spend the next few days and

The Unbearable Heaviness of Stephen Seagull.

weeks while he recuperated writing the script for a film that would tell the story exactly as it had happened.

Six months had passed since the incident, and Stephen was hard at work filming Cop Warrior, his self-penned film based on the events of that night. They had already filmed a large part of the film, showing the police approaching him to join, the weeks he spent training his colleagues how to fight properly and the correct way to shoot, and now tonight they were filming the centrepiece, the night where he saved his partner from certain death at the hands of a vicious drug gang.

"Aaaaaaaaaaaand...scene".

As the director called for action Big Stevie set his jaw firmly, putting on his war face. They were in the patrol car, and he soothed his slightly anxious partner as they drove around the mean streets.

Suddenly the radio crackled "huge gang disturbance at Rosomond Street, please investigate with extreme caution".

"Affirmative, we're on our way" Big Stevie answered, turning to his partner. "let's roll".

"M...maybe we should wait for back up Stephen, I'm frightened".

Big Stevie laid a comforting hand on his poor partner's shoulder soothingly.

"It's okay Sam, I'll look after you".

"Th...thanks Stephen, you're the greatest cop I've ever known".

"Yes. Yes I am".

They arrived at the scene of the disturbance soon after, a massive, fortified mansion on the edge of town, with turrets on every corner of the surrounding brick walls. In these turrets stood armed men, with machine guns in their hands (see, I told you they were armed).

"How the hell are we supposed to get in there?" Sam asked, voice quivering.

Big Stevie chuckled, and got out of the car.

"Leave that to me Sam, leave that to me".

He walked around to the back of the car, and got out a foldaway trampoline. Spreading it out on the grass, he turned to his puzzled partner.

"Maybe it would be for the best if you stayed here in the car; leave this to the expert".

Sam breathed a sigh of relief.

"Wow thanks Stephen, you're the best".

Sam scurried back into the car, and the camera pulled back far enough away that hopefully no-one would notice that it clearly wasn't Big Stevie doing the next bit. Big Stevie's stuntman ran at full speed, hit the trampoline and flew waaaaaaaaaaaaaaaay up into the air, flying over the turret below, with its unsuspecting (probably Russian) baddie. Big Stevie('s stuntman) landed on the lawn on the other side

The Unbearable Heaviness of Stephen Seagull.

and drew his gun, scanning the scene with an expert eye. He counted seventeen thugs dotted around, but thankfully none of them had spotted him. He crept up to a bush near the front door, a door guarded by two large gentlemen. Reaching into his top pocket he pulled out a mint, and threw it behind them. They turned towards the sound and as they did so Big Stevie pounced, knocking them both out with one punch (not one punch per person, but two men with a SINGLE punch). He tried the door but it was locked, but he spotted an open window at the top of the mansion. In one swift movement Big Stevie('s stuntman) scaled the front of the building and acrobatically threw himself through the open window. Three drug dealers in the room turned around, startled, but before they could raise either their guns or the alarm he had quickly and efficiently choked each one out. He grabbed two of the AK-47s in each hand, and went out into the hallway. A hail of bullets thudded into the woodwork around him and he dove behind a plant pot, returning fire and felling four anonymous thugs. Two more thugs on motorbikes roared up the stairs, firing shotguns at Big Stevie, but he managed to evade their fire and jumped right on the first bike, punching the rider, sending him flying into the air and landing on the bike behind him, sending both of the men and the bike crashing down the stairs. Big Stevie threw one of the Ak-47s away and grabbed the throttle of the bike, pulled a wheelie at the top of the stairs, turned around and drove straight back down again to the lower floor. Various thugs came bursting out of doors brandishing guns as he drove along the hallway, but he expertly shot them all before skidding to a halt on the plush carpet in front of a large, open door. He got off the bike and slowly advanced towards the door, raising the AK-47.

"Okay hombre," he shouted coolly into the darkness of the room. "Come out with your hands up and I'll let you live".

Two figures appeared from the gloom, a swarthy gentleman digging a rifle into the back of a naked, nubile young woman.

"Get out of my way, or she dies".

"Now don't do anything hasty" Big Stevie said softly. "We can sort this out in a nice manner, nobody needs to get hurt".

"Nobody needs to get hurt? You've just killed twenty-three of my best men! And all without a single mark on you; you really are an amazing and noble fighter. Unfortunately as much as I respect you for your martial skills, I intend to get out of here and onto my escape yacht, so drop the gun, now!".

He shoved the gun harshly into the woman's back, causing her tits to jiggle a bit in a sexy manner.

"NOW!"

"Okay, calm down" Big Stevie said, gently laying the AK-47 down on the ground. He stood back up with his hands in the air. "Now come on, just let the woman go and I'll let you walk out of here a free man".

"Ain't gonna happen big guy".

"I was afraid you were going to say that".

As soon as the words had left Big Stevie's lips he kicked his leg up towards the man, and his boot flew off and went through the air, hitting the man perfectly in the face. The man was knocked off his feet and

The Unbearable Heaviness of Stephen Seagull.

fell back into the room, and Big Stevie threw the woman out of the way and jumped on top of him, punching him repeatedly until there was no longer any resistance. He got up and approached the woman, taking off his jacket and wrapping it around her because, as well as being one of the hardest men in the world, he was also a completely chivalrous gentleman, with a lot of respect for the strumpets.

"There there, you're safe now little girl".

She looked up at her saviour, and fell into his arms, and as they embraced their lips locked in a passionate kiss.

"Aaaaaaaaaaaand...cut".

The scene had gone perfectly, and though it wasn't perhaps EXACTLY as it had happened in real life, Big Stevie had strived to make it as realistic as possible, with any slight tweaks simply there to try and fit the story into the two and a half hours that the film was to last for.

He accidently knocked the jacket back off the young girl and had another quick look at her paps, and then retire to his trailer, happy that another classic film was soon to be added to the collection.

The Unbearable Heaviness of Stephen Seagull.

The film opened to reviews ("I take it there are no fitness tests to be a policeman anymore?"-The Paris Syndrome; "The end credits were in a lovely font"-Leicester Bugle; "Has anyone seen his eyes?"-Los Angeles Burgling Monthly; "Do policemen really sit THAT much?"-The Dundee Herald), though yet again there were vicious rumours from certain quarters that Big Stevie had embellished the truth somewhat, and things may not have happened quite like they did in the film. These accusations came from many sources around the world, just like they had every other time one of his films had been released, or he had done an interview where he'd regaled the host and audience with stories from his fascinating past as a hired assassin, special forces hero, war-astronaut etc., but he was pretty sure that the real source of all these rumours each and every time was Billy Thompson, an ex-postie of his who Big Stevie had forgotten to tip one Christmas.

Things took a turn for the worse for poor Big Stevie when his wife left him, and he realised he would have to do his own washing again. He had no idea why she had left as the lazy cow had never bothered to learn English, and it wasn't like he was going to learn fuckin' RUSSIAN. Luckily he had made her sign a pre-nup on their wedding day and most of his stuff was rented nowadays anyway, so it didn't really cost him financially apart from the cost of her plane ticket back to Russia. She had also signed a contract saying that she would be paying this back (one of the best things about marrying foreign chicks who don't speak your lingo Big Stevie thought, was that you could get them to sign any old shit, and they hadn't a clue).

He decided to try online dating as that seemed to be all the rage nowadays, and so sat down one afternoon and filled out his profile on Match.com:

"Handsome man seeks beautiful woman, intelligence unimportant. Powerfully-built real man looking for a woman who understands the instructions on a washing machine, and will do her duty in the bedroom when demanded. I am an incredibly well-travelled polymath, with stories that will blow your pretty little mind, and in the interests of equality I would be just as interested in hearing your stories too, in a ten minute "lady-time" slot to be agreed between us upon meeting (one or two minutes may be added or subtracted to/from this depending on your attractiveness). I am a very good catch so you would be expected to match up, and should I deign to date you I would insist upon weighing you every morning, with heavy fines for any weight gain over an acceptable two-pound rise. I am 40 (ish), but probably look around 28, maybe 29 on a really bad day. I am looking for a woman in the 19-27 age range, though I would consider someone older (possibly even early thirties!) should the breasts be humungous. Don't worry if you don't have your own vacuum as one can be provided, but I would expect you to go halves on the date, as women are equal and all that bollocks. Look forward to hearing from you, and you will definitely look forward to seeing me".

He put up four photos of himself when he was in his early twenties, as he presumed that he looked pretty much the same now as he did then, apart from maybe putting on a pound or two, and waited for his inbox to be inundated.

By the end of the week he had over one replies, and had sent out four thousand three hundred and seventy-six "likes", messages, and dick pics. He had arranged a couple of dates for that weekend, and was really looking forward to finally getting some hoovering done, and possibly a blowjob.

The Unbearable Heaviness of Stephen Seagull.

That Saturday night he was sitting in a restaurant with one of his dates, Jennifer. The restaurant (her pick) was a bit expensive for his tastes (and wallet) but they were going halves, and he had managed to sell some of his ex-wife's old underwear to the creepy man at the end of the street, so he was feeling a bit flush. Jennifer was a tall blonde, twenty-five, and worked as a model. She had walked right past him initially outside the restaurant, and had seemed a bit surprised when she finally realised who he was. She had muttered something about him looking a lot different to his pictures, but he knew that this was just nerves on her part, and that she was well up for it. As they tucked into their starters (Waldorf salad for her, Steak, chips, roast potatoes, fries, sausages, crinkle cut chips, Heinz baked beans, curly fries, and a tomato for him), he decided that he may as well pretend to give a shit about what she did etc.

"So, what do you do Jennifer?"

"Um, I've already told you that I'm a model Stephen".

"Oh yeah, sorry. So do you travel a lot for that?"

"Oh yes, I go all over the world, it's really exciting and I meet so many different people from all over the world".

"Yes, I've been all over the world too, my passport has more stamps on it than…um…someone else's passport who has been travelling a hell of a lot. Like yours, perhaps. So you're a model, you must see a lot of your colleagues naked then?"

"Well yes, I suppose I do, but after a while it just becomes part of the job, and not weird or anything. So what do you do yourself Stephen?".

"He laughed, "Well as you are a chick I can forgive you for not knowing who I am, but in the world of men's entertainment let's just say that I am a huge deal".

"You work in porn? I have to say, I'm not comfortable about that".

"No, not porn, though I could do that no problem" He winked at her, and she shuddered. "No, I own my own film company, also writing, starring and executive producing as well, with the emphasise on starring. If you have any men in your family they will be bowing at my feet when they meet me, you can be sure of that".

"If they meet you Stephen, let's not get ahead of ourselves".

"Oh come on, why on earth would you not want to continue our relationship?"

"This isn't a relationship Stephen, It's a date! I mean, I'm not being rude, but you do look a lot different from your photos, and you're a lot older than you claim in your bio as well. I'm sure you would be a nice catch for someone of my mother's age, but I'm looking for someone nearer my own ".

"You would rather a weak little boy over a real man? Have you seen the so-called men in your generation? Weak, soft, little-biceped, mascara-wearing girly-boys who would literally be frightened to death if they had seen even a quarter of what I had back in 'Nam. I remember saying to Bruce Lee when he came to me for some training that eventually the pair of us were going to run out of sparring partners, as they're not making men anymore".

The Unbearable Heaviness of Stephen Seagull.

"Well at least the dinosaurs didn't go extinct as previously thought, so that might make up for the death of men" she tutted, rolling her eyes.

"Look, never mind all that, I don't want to argue or it will spoil the sex later, so let's change the subject: what's your favourite type of num-chuks?"

"Stephen, I have no idea what that is, and just for your information there isn't going to be any sex later on, nor any other time. I'm sure you're a nice guy, in your own, weird way, but I have absolutely no interest in sleeping with a man old enough to be my grandad, and who is perhaps not as slender as my usual type".

"You don't like muscle? What woman doesn't like a muscular athletic man? And for another thing I could be your slightly older brother, tops, and trust me you would love the incest".

"Oh I like muscle Stephen, I just don't want to spend three hours searching for it underneath all that blubber. Look, no offence but this isn't working, I think I'm going to cut my losses and go home".

She got up from the table.

"Where are you going?" Stephen spluttered, spraying fries everywhere "we haven't even had the main course yet! I was looking forward to dessert! Look, sit down, I'm sure we can salvage something from the night if we just reach some kind of a compromise, maybe a hand-job in the bogs or something?"

She stormed off, leaving Stephen sitting alone with the eyes of the other diners burning into him.

"Hey!" he shouted, "we were supposed to go halves on the bill!"

The Unbearable Heaviness of Stephen Seagull.

After that dead-end date with that young woman and her ridiculous demands, Big Stevie could have been deterred, but he was made of sterner stuff, and soon he had another date lined up. He had picked the (much cheaper) place to dine this time, just in case, and as they sat down on the bench outside Gary's Burger Van he looked at his date admiringly. She was twenty-four, brunette, and owned her own car! Big Stevie marvelled at the world we live in now, where a mere woman can own a car while a man as great as he was could only rent one. He was also renting the clothes and shoes he was wearing on the date, so would have to be careful not to spill any ketchup on himself during the date.

Frustratingly, like Jennifer she hadn't seemed to recognise her date as he sat there waving at her, and a look that could almost have been mistaken for extreme disappointment had crossed her face, if you didn't know better.

"Er…hello, Stephen?"

"Yes, that's me" he smiled, not getting up from the bench.

"I'm Emma, it's, er, nice to meet you".

She sat down, moving his burger box out of the way.

"Nice to meet you too Emma, would you like something to eat?"

She looked at the greasy, dirty burger van doubtfully.

"I am quite hungry to be honest, but I'm not sure if I trust eating something from there".

"No, honestly, Gary is great. I know it doesn't look like much but the food is well worth it; go on, try something".

"Oh okay then, maybe a burger".

"Great! While you're up there, get me a double cheeseburger and fries will you? Thanks".

He made no attempt to offer her any money, and she sighed and walked to the van. After a few minutes she returned with their food, and sat down on the cleanest looking bit of the bench.

"You look a little…different from your pictures Stephen, no offence".

"Yes, I think my ponytail was a bit shorter when they were taken" he replied, spraying her with cheeseburger.

She said nothing, just stared at his belly.

"So, which type of kick is your favourite?"

"Sorry?"

"I said which type of kick is your favourite?, you know, in martial arts".

"Oh, well I'm not actually into martial arts Stephen, though I do go to the gym".

The Unbearable Heaviness of Stephen Seagull.

"Of course of course, you're a woman, sometimes I forget just how silly you all are. I'm something of a master in martial arts, probably in the top two in the entire world (he knew he was actually number one, but didn't want to appear arrogant)".

"Oh that's nice. As I say I do exercise, weights and running mostly, but I don't do any fighting".

Stephen burst out into raucous laughter.

"Weights? But you're a woman! Oh, you could be almost funny, for a chick" he said, wiping tears from his eyes.

"I do weights Stephen, and so do a lot of women nowadays; maybe if you had set foot in a gym in the last forty years you would know this".

She stared blatantly at his belly again.

"I don't need to go to a gym Emma, I'm lucky to be naturally fit and muscular. Anyway, I did so much martial arts training over the years that I no longer need to train, my body is a machine, primed for action always".

A two-minute silence followed, Emma staring at his belly the entire time, before she finally broke the silence.

"So, have you been single long Stephen?"

"No, not long, unsurprisingly. I was married until very recently, but decided that though she was still utterly obsessed with me that I was no longer in love with her, and dumped her. She still messages me every day, but I've moved on and I'm ready for the next lucky lady to enjoy my attentions. Play your cards right, and it could be you".

"Um, well, it's early days yet Stephen. I'm not in any hurry to form a relationship just yet, I'm just seeing what is out there before making any decision".

He chuckled. "Well there's not really going to be much point in looking after meeting me surely? You're only going to be going down market after me, so if I'm not what you want then maybe celibacy is the only way to go for you. Are you going to eat the rest of that burger?"

"No, you can have it. Look to be honest Stephen what I just said isn't entirely true, I AM hoping to meet someone to form a lasting relationship with on this dating site, but, and I'm sorry to say this, you aren't quite in my age range. I'm looking for someone nearer my own age, and your photographs on the site led me to believe that this was the case. To be honest when you contacted me I still wasn't sure after reading your bio, but I figured that there was nothing to lose meeting you for one date".

Stephen glared at her angrily.

"You chicks are all the same, so shallow and looks-orientated! Yes, I may be a couple of years older than in those photos, give or take, and possibly an ounce or two heavier, but I defy you to find anyone who has aged as little or as well as I have! Most women would love to have a sexy, slightly-older gentleman on their arm, to show off to their jealous friends. If I wanted to be critical then I could easily make a few

The Unbearable Heaviness of Stephen Seagull.

comments about the way that YOU look, such as your slightly saggy breasts, or those thunder-thighs of yours, maybe point out that googly eye of yours, but no, I'm far too much of a gentleman to reduce you to mere looks. Maybe you should learn something from me, and then you might get a bit more luck in the porking department".

She got up and walked away.

"What is it with you women nowadays", he shouted at her retreating figure. "Don't you like real men any longer?"

He was now really angry, and only a banana thick-shake was going to quell the fire inside him now.

The Unbearable Heaviness of Stephen Seagull.

Big Stevie decided that American women were too spoiled nowadays, and had been fooled by the soft Western Media into believing that those young girly-boys prevalent everywhere were what passed for men, so it would be best to look elsewhere. He thought about trying Russia again, but after that last wife (whatever her name was) he was a bit put off by the idea, so instead he ordered a mail-order bride from Mongolia, for a very reasonable price.

Two weeks later she came in the mail, Big Stevie signed for her, and took her into the front porch and unwrapped her. He smiled as he looked her up and down: she was curvy in all the right places, and had an attractive, twenty-two-year-old face. She could do with smiling a bit he thought to himself, but that would surely come once she had settled into her fantastic new life with this hunk of studly beef. He looked at the instruction leaflet that came with her to see what her name was, but it was one of those ridiculous hard-to-pronounce foreign names, so he decided that she was now called Susan Seagull.

"Hello Susan".

She looked at him, confused.

"I said, HELLO SUSAN".

She looked at him, still with that puzzled look on her face.

"Oh never mind, just come with me".

He led her into the house, sighing at the amount of time it took her to struggle in with her heavy luggage, and pointed to the kettle.

"Coffee, yes?"

She looked at the kettle, looked back at him, and looked at the kettle again.

"YOU MAKE COFFEE YES?" This was going to be hard work...Hopefully later on, she would pick up the meaning of "touch that" a bit quicker than she was picking this up. All this standing up was tiring, so he went through and flopped down on the sofa, flicking through the channels in the hope of finding one of his films on one of the channels. He realised it was a bit early for one of his hard-hitting art-pieces to be on, so put on one of his own DVDs. Eventually Susan came through with two cups of coffee, and sat down next to him. It was a bit forward of her, but he would let it pass. For now.

Get Thee Behind Me Santa started on the screen, and Big Stevie pointed at the screen, then pointed at himself, smiling and nodding. She looked at the TV, looked at him, and shrugged. She had BETTER have soft hands, he thought to himself wearily.

Around half an hour passed, and Big Stevie's character had just garrotted an elf with his own belt, when she suddenly started screaming in glee, pointing excitedly at the screen.

"HIPPO YOU! HIPPO YOU!"

"That's not a hi...oh forget it, at least you're finally getting the message. ME, BIG STAR, YOU, LUCKY WOMAN, YES?"

"You rich TV hippo man?"

The Unbearable Heaviness of Stephen Seagull.

"I do okay" he sighed, thinking it was probably for the best not to mention that the coffee cups and the kettle were rented, and the sugar and coffee were on hire purchase.

"Passport?"

"Now don't you worry about that Susan, I'm going to look after that for you, but it will be safely tucked away in an impenetrable safe ready for whenever you want it; I promise. Now, do you know how to load a dishwasher?"

The Unbearable Heaviness of Stephen Seagull.

The next morning he left her locked in the house with her left hand sellotaped to the vacuum, hoping she would have figured it out by the time he got home. He had initially thought about also testing to see how good she could cook, but then thought that might have to wait for another day, and they could get a takeaway just for tonight.

Cough.

As he drove to the film set to begin filming his latest film, Black Steel, in which he would play an African-American welder who used to be in the special forces, he felt better than he had for a long while. Susan was going to be a work in progress, but she was attractive, obedient, and he would have her paid off by the end of March, and then he would own her outright. His fee for Black Steel was enough that he was considering maybe splashing out on a small honeymoon for him and his new bride, which would just so happen to be to London, where he'd received a very attractive offer to star in a film; an offer which didn't quite stretch to covering the flight over.

He strolled onto set, basking in the admiration of the crew and co-stars. The boot-polish had been applied, and his ponytail had been woven into a very fetching set of dreadlocks. At the risk of coming across as a bit arrogant, he reckoned that he was better at being a black man than anyone else in the world, including those who had a head-start by being born black. He picked up the gun, and walked to his mark, ready to begin filming today's scene.

"Action".

"Wagwan Bredren" His character, Ignatius Palpatine said to the four prisoners tied up in the warehouse in front of him. His crew stood ominously behind him, guns at the ready.

"You are going to give me the information I need about the drug shipment, or my friends and I are going to get very creative with some power tools, ya dig?"

The men said nothing, though one of them spat at the floor in front of Ignatius. He said nothing, but walked over and cracked the man in the face with the butt of his gun, and the man slumped forward, out for the count.

"Now den" Ignatius said, eyeballing the other three threateningly, "Anyone else got some ting ta say?"

Silence.

"Okay den, who wants ta tells me about da shipment den? You?" He went right up to the face of one of the men, who stared defiantly, and kept silent.

Ignatius smiled, and walked over to a briefcase. Opening it he took out a cleaver, pair of pliers, and a drill. He walked back to the men and pressed play on a stereo system just beside them. Buffalo Soldier by Bob Marley began to fill the room with sound, and he pulled the trigger on the drill as he crouched down to the first man.

"Irie".

"Cut".

The Unbearable Heaviness of Stephen Seagull.

With the scene in the bag, all was good. Well, apart from the actor who was still knocked out by the butt of the gun.

The director Ralph Waterstone approached Big Stevie meekly. He wasn't keen on criticising Big Stevie as Ralph had been very lucky to get this job after Big Stevie objected to having someone called RALPH directing such a manly picture, but something needed to be said.

"Er…Stephen, sorry to trouble you but can I have a word?"

"As long as that word is Stephen you were awesome in that scene, then yes, you can". Big Stevie laughed uproariously at his clever joke, and Ralph decided it was probably for the best not to point out the flaw in his witty repartee.

"Great one Stephen, but no, I need to talk to you about your, um, heavy-handedness when dealing with other actors and crew".

"What do you mean?"

"Look Stephen, I know that we're filming an action film and there are some real tough guys on set, but at the end of the day we ARE just acting, and some of your violence needs to be a lot more restrained. Acting is all about pretending, and you need to pretend to hit your co-stars, not actually do it at full-force".

"First things first I have to correct you on something you said, there is ONE tough guy on set, and that is me. Secondly if they aren't man enough to take the occasional hit then it's not my problem that they are pussy little boy-men. For the record I DO pull my punches, if a trained killer like me punched one of these Nancy-boy actors for real I would kill them, which would look great for the film, but would leave a mess for the cleaners to have to sort out".

"If it was the occasional, accidental hit then it wouldn't be so bad Stephen but it's all the time! You didn't need to actually hit Tom with the rifle butt, there was no need to make contact at all with the filming techniques we have nowadays. Now Tom is having to go to hospital and if we are really unlucky he will sue the company, and we can't afford that".

"Don't worry, I'll visit him tomorrow and "have a word"; he won't do shit".

"It's not just Tom though Stephen, there are constant whispers in the film world about actors and stuntmen complaining about their time working on your films, and the bruises they got on them. I'm just asking you to not actually make contact, just to PRETEND to hit them, and maybe stop spitting at the stuntmen when you walk past them in the canteen all the time".

"You don't ask a tiger to stop being a tiger, but okay, I'll TRY not to make your soft little actors and stuntmen cry. I tell you, none of them would have lasted five minutes back with me in 'Nam".

"I didn't know you were in Vietnam Stephen?"

"Huh, there are a lot of things you don't know about me Ralph, you name a war that happened since the early fifties and I can guarantee that I was there working in a top-secret capacity, and let's just say that many of these conflicts wouldn't have stopped when they did if I hadn't intervened".

The Unbearable Heaviness of Stephen Seagull.

"Okay, well anyway if you could just try and be a bit gentler with your colleagues that would be great".

"Okay Ralph, no problem. As an animal lover I will endeavour to be kinder to those pussies".

The Unbearable Heaviness of Stephen Seagull.

Black Steel opened to a bit of a furore and got Big Stevie's name back into the media, albeit for the wrong reasons. He went onto various chat shows to explain that the misunderstanding was simply due to the rest of the world being stupid and him being far better educated than they are, but unfortunately they were too stupid to understand his eloquently argued point, and the film suffered as a result. There were accusations that he was a racist bigot stuck in the past, but if that was the case then why would he have bought a FOREIGN woman? Their arguments fell down every time he challenged them cleverly, but despite him PROVING that the Bob Marley CD was his own and telling them how much he loved Indian food, some weak-willed people still believed the vicious slurs, and he retreated from public life for a while to let it all simmer down. He realised that this would be the perfect time to go over to London and take them up on that film offer, as England was still stuck in Tudor times and therefore would have very little media to spread their lies (if Hollywood was true to life, and he had no reason to doubt it).

Susan seemed really excited to leave the house for the first time in five months, and she seemed so happy that he felt a little bit guilty, and wished that he had paid for her to fly first class with him as well. Still, she was probably fine way back there, and it meant that he could stare at the air hostess's arses without her disapproving glare.

They reached London and he was surprised to see streetlights, and signs of electricity all around. As he patiently waited at the taxi rank for his wife to come with the luggage, he realised that maybe London was a bit more advanced than he had thought, and maybe they WOULD have a MacDonald's after all.

Eventually she got there, and they entered a taxi.

"Cor blimey guvna, that 'otel's a right crock of Eartha Kitt and no mistake" the driver said, as he pulled out into traffic (traffic! Big Stevie marvelled, London is SO different to what I thought), "Daahn't you want to take your woman somewhere a bit nicer?"

"The film company are paying for the hotel, not me, so I didn't have much say in the matter. Worst comes to worst I can send her out for cleaning supplies and tidy the room up a bit; I can take the money out of her food budget, or she can pay me back at a later date".

"Well it's your funeral guvna. Film company eh? Are you an actor or sumfink?"

Big Stevie chuckled.

"You might say that...you might also say that I'm the biggest action star in the world".

The driver turned around with a surprised look on his face.

"Nah, The Rock, in my cab! Wow, wait 'til I tell the lads! I must say though, you look a bit...different in real life, your muscles look a lot more...relaxed".

"No, don't be stupid, I would break him into tiny pieces!"

"Sly?"

"No! try again, and THINK about it".

The Unbearable Heaviness of Stephen Seagull.

"Dolph Lundgren?"

"STEPHEN SEAGULL!"

"Who?"

"STEPHEN SEAGULL! You must have heard of me! I was in Prophet of Rage!"

"Never 'eard of it guvna".

"Tell Satan I'm Coming, And I'm Bringing the Boys?"

"Nah".

"Gluteus Maximus?"

"Nope".

"Hammer of Russia?"

"Wee Doogie Crunchfist?"

"Colonel Death?"

"Feel My Elbow Cocksucka?"

"Skulduggery and Commie Buggery?"

"Ninja Burger?"

"Punch My Face Beeyatch?"

(23 minutes later)

"Maverick Detective?"

"Walk Alone?"

"My Bazooka, Your Anus?"

"Vikings With Machine-Guns?"

"Trapped on a Big Ship?"

"Yes! I know that one! Cor, that girl in the birthday cake had a right set of hot n' cold taps n' no mistake!"

"There was more to the film than that" Big Stevie sighed.

"Yeah, probably. Anyway, here we are".

They pulled up outside a crumbling, dirty-looking dive of a hotel. Scruffy little urchins scampered about the street, plump housewives hanging out washing on lines in the gardens, fags in mouths, a chimney

The Unbearable Heaviness of Stephen Seagull.

sweep whistling as he led his horse and cart down the street, and an elderly gentleman ushered some little homeless children into his house for some warm soup. Probably.

"I wouldn't be out 'ere after dark if I were you, luv a duck, cor blimey etc". The taxi driver said, as he snacked on some jellied eels.

"Huh, the only thing to fear around here after dark will be ME" Big Stevie said, as he loaded Susan up with the luggage.

"Well fair enough guv, hope you enjoy your stay in laaavley ol' Lahndan Town, apples and pears, I love our dear old queen, and so forth". He drove away, the sound of Chas N' Dave on his stereo fading into the distance as he disappeared over the horizon. Or around the next bend.

"Well Susan, here we are, our home for the next few weeks".

She didn't exactly look impressed, but he was sure that she would like it better once they were settled into their room. He entered the building and approached the front desk. He rang the bell. Nothing. He waited a few moments and then rang to again. Nothing. This continued for a good few minutes until eventually a bored teenager came through from a door behind the desk, chewing gum and staring at her phone.

"Yeah?" she said, not taking her eyes off the phone.

"I have a room booked in under the name Seagull. Stephen Seagull". He waited for the inevitable gushing from a young fan, but nothing. Presumably her phone didn't show films.

"Yeah, I see it here, room 37, right at the top of the stairs on your left".

"Do you have an elevator?"

"A lift? Why, don't you have working legs fat-boy?"

"Excuse me?"

"Oh, fat AND deaf, you're quite a catch Mr. no-eyes".

"How dare you! I'm a paying customer! You can't talk to me like that! If you were a man I'd kick your ass little girl".

"I bet you can't wipe your own arse though fat boy, probably get out of breath thinking".

"I demand to speak to the manager, right now!"

"Alright, calm down sweaty cheeks, dad's away so you can't speak to him just now. Why don't you chill out and go up to your room before you have a heart attack? If you can't manage the stairs all in one go you can stop halfway up for a rest and I'll get a blanket sent up to you".

"Rest assured, I WILL be talking to your father. In the meantime do you have someone to take my bags up?"

The Unbearable Heaviness of Stephen Seagull.

"Fuck sake, no wonder you're the size you are!" She opened the door behind her again and shouted "GEORGE! GEORGE! Get your arse through here now!"

"He'll just be a moment, SIR".

Susan came crashing in through the door, buried under a mountain of luggage. She flopped down onto a chair, gasping for breath.

The young teen looked at her, looked at Big Stevie, but said nothing. An elderly gentleman, around eighty years old, came shuffling through the door behind the teen, and leant against the counter for support, breathing heavily.

"George, this...gentleman would like you to take his luggage up to his room for him, as his hands are broken or something".

The old man shuffled veeeeeerrrrryyyyyy slowly around the counter towards the luggage, still holding onto the counter with each step.

Big Stevie went to him, carefully taking his arm.

"Woah there old-timer, take it easy. I don't expect you to take all my luggage up the stairs for me, I'm not a monster". He took three of the smaller bags and loaded them onto the old man, whose knees buckled slightly and trembled.

"Susan here will help you, and you can make a few trips if there's too much for the pair of you to take all at once. Just be careful with that bag in your left hand though, as my new slow cooker is in there and I don't want you to drop it".

He turned to the young woman, "is there any food on the go?"

"No, it's bed and breakfast only I'm afraid, though you can phone for a takeaway if you want and eat it in your room; I don't give a shit".

"Do you have any menus for the local takeaways, little miss hostess with the mostest?"

She reached into a drawer and flung a few leaflets onto the counter.

"Help yourself chunks, though I think you've had enough already".

He glowered at her, picked up the leaflets and walked up the stairs. He went into their room: a gloomy, squalid looking little cupboard, with hardly enough room to swing a cat, should that be your thing. The film company hadn't exactly pulled out all the stops for their visiting superstar, he thought bitterly. As he ordered a Chinese takeaway over the phone plus an Indian chaser (Susan probably wasn't hungry, he assumed), he thought to himself that he was really going to have to have words with the director of the film.

He lay back on the bed, his feet aching after a long day of walking around airports. As he heard Susan and George huffing and puffing up the stairs he wished she would hurry up, so she could take his boots off for him and massage his poor, tender feet.

The Unbearable Heaviness of Stephen Seagull.

Big Stevie got a taxi the next day to meet the film director, Percival Fortescue-Buckingham-Farquhar, and discuss the new project: American Animal in London (England). He was to play Brex Hanningham, an American mercenary hired to help the indigenous population fight the Norman invaders in 1066. In the film he would lead (of course) a small band of renegade warriors (Robin Hood, King Arthur, Boudicca, and some disposable extras), put together to spearhead a secret mission into enemy territory and kill William.

"Hello Stephen, a pleasure to make your acquaintance" Percival rose from behind his desk, and extended his hand.

"Hello Percival, the pleasure is all mine. Well, probably half n' half if I'm being honest, maybe 75/25% in your favour".

"So, raring to go Stephen?"

"Yeah, I just wanted to go over a few things, I had some ideas to improve the film a bit".

"Well it's a bit late in the day for any drastic changes, but I'm willing to listen".

"I was thinking that my character could wear a cowboy hat, as a subtle nod to his American roots".

"No, I don't think that would look right amongst all the armour etc. Stephen, but a good idea though, just not quite right for this project".

"I think you're wrong, but you're the boss I suppose, technically. Okay well another idea I had was to have a romance between me and Boudicca; I presume you've cast a hot bit of skirt for the role?"

"Actually we have cast someone with fighting skills in mind, a martial arts expert just getting into acting. We weren't planning on having any romantic sub-plot with her character, we wanted to focus on her as a warrior, and her being the equal of the men".

"Ha! Good one! I love that dry British sense of humour of yours! But seriously, there's not much point in casting a woman if she's not going to get off with the main star at some point, is there?"

"Um, you're not actually the main star in this picture Stephen, sorry to say. In the interests of equality and the fact that we now live in the twenty-first century we're trying to shy away from having women as mere sex objects Stephen, her character is one of the main leads in the film, and she is respected for her leadership and military acumen every bit as much as her male colleagues".

"More of your British wit, very good. Who the hell do you have in this film that's a bigger star than me?"

"This is an ensemble piece Stephen, it's not about who is bigger than whom, I've managed to gather together a quality cast who are all respected in the field of acting, but who have perhaps fallen from public view over the past few years. I think of this film as a chance to get these names back where they belong in the limelight again. Plus, you were all nice and cheap".

Big Stevie was livid, his face burning bright red, and not just from the effort of holding his gut in.

The Unbearable Heaviness of Stephen Seagull.

"You cast Stephen Seagull in your picture and don't give him top billing! What kind of madness is that? Do you realise how big I am in certain areas of the world? I really think you should concentrate the film on my character, especially as I'll be outshining everyone else anyway with my star wattage".

"I'm sorry Stephen but the film is already written and it stays as it is. Unfortunately you have already signed your contract so whether you like it or not you will have to honour it, and film the film the way that we intend".

Big Stevie sighed.

"I am a man of honour and so I will indeed do as requested, but I think you're making a big mistake. Can't you at least bend towards the cowboy hat thing?"

"No, sorry Stephen, we want this film to be historically accurate, and a cowboy hat would be anachronistic in this time period".

"But I'm still doing it in a Texan accent though?"

"Yes of course, he's still American".

The Unbearable Heaviness of Stephen Seagull.

Big Stevie was standing on a cold moor, shivering despite the onesie. The rest of the cast were milling around nearby, and he looked at them with barely concealed contempt. King Arthur was past it, Robin Hood looked like he couldn't fight his way out of a paper bag, and Boudicca was wearing a shapeless uniform which didn't show any cleavage whatsoever. If this was real life he would definitely be the leader of this sorry shower, he thought to himself bitterly. Of course if this had been real life then he would have kicked Norman ass, and they would never have conquered this sorry little land, but unfortunately for England he had been born too late to save them. Better luck next time English people.

"Okay everyone, get ready please."

Big Stevie removed the onesie, and climbed upon his horse (with a little help from three extras). He cantered carefully towards the rest of the band of heroes, not being too keen on horses (not scared, fuck RIGHT off with that, just not a fan).

"Okay, action!"

So Boudicca, you have somehow managed to capture one of the Normans? You, a woman? Did someone help you?"

"Stephen" Percival interjected "No adlibbing please, stick to the script".

Big Stevie tutted quietly, but did as he was told.

"So Boudicca, you have managed to capture one of the Normans, well done! We can interrogate him and find out their weaknesses, maybe find a way into their camp and kill William".

"I have him tied up in my tent" Boudicca replied, "come this way".

"Tied up eh? Planning to have your wicked way with him in a prolonged and graphic scene are you, you sexy bitch?"

"Stephen, what did I just say about adlibbing? Please, just say what is in your script!"

Big Stevie tutted again, this time louder.

"Okay Percival, whatever you say. Let's go Boudicca".

He, Boudicca, Robin Hood and King Arthur plus two faceless extras trotted towards her tent. They entered, and saw a muscular, topless man tied to a rack".

"Why is he topless when you wouldn't entertain my idea to have Boudicca fight topless Percival?"

"Not now Stephen!"

Robin approached the Norman warrior, who looked at the small group with pure hatred.

"Hello, my name is Robin, do you understand me?"

"Yes, I understand you, English pig!" The man replied, in a heavy Russian accent.

"Good, that's incredibly handy. If what you tell us helps us to end this invasion then you will not be harmed, but otherwise..."

The Unbearable Heaviness of Stephen Seagull.

"I will tell you nothing, schweinhund!"

"Oh that is a shame old boy, looks like we will have to torture you horribly then. Arthur, bring the tools will you, there's a good chap".

"No problem chum" said Arthur, as he approached with a large, heavy chest. He took out a hammer and handed it to Robin.

Robin looked the Norman in the eye, smiling.

"Now are you sure you wish to keep quiet?"

The Norman spat at Robin, who wiped it away with a bit of an extra's uniform.

"Okay, then, so be it". Robin smashed the hammer down onto the bare toes of the Norman, who shrieked out in agony. Robin raised the hammer again.

"GOTT IN HIMMEL! PLEASE, STOP! I'll tell you what you want!" the Norman sobbed, like a big baby.

"That's more like it" Robin said, wiping the blood from the hammer and handing it back to Arthur. "Now, how many of you are there?"

"I don't know" the Norman said, "being a simple medieval soldier I can only count up to five, so I'll say at least five".

"Wise guy huh?" Brex said, moving out of the shadows at the back of the tent.

"No, I'm saying that I'm the opposite of a wise guy, I'm thick as pig-shit".

Brex knelt down, right up close to the Norman.

"Okay then, how closely-guarded is your king?"

"Oh not at all, we tend to leave our leaders on a hill by themselves, with torches surrounding them and a big arrow pointing to them for any enemies to see".

Brex slapped him hard across the face.

"Tell us what we need to know wise guy, or the hammer comes out again!"

"Okay okay, chill out dude. Our king is very heavily-guarded with at least five of the best warriors we have surrounding him at all times. I don't think you stand much chance of infiltrating our defences and killing him if that is your plan, especially with such a small band".

"This isn't any old band of soldiers though dear fellow" Arthur said, "what you see here are some of the best fighters in the whole of England, plus the best kick-ass mutha from the US in Brex here. We can kill your king no problem, elite guard or no elite guard".

"Yeah," Brex said, "we can destroy anyone who tries to stand in our way, even WITH a girl in our ranks".

"Stephen!" Percival shouted, angrily.

The Unbearable Heaviness of Stephen Seagull.

"Sorry".

"Is William tough, will he give us any resistance?" Boudicca asked.

"Ha, he would kill all of you with one hand tied behind his back. He's a REAL warrior, not like you little dummkopfs".

Brex punched him hard in the face, and followed it up with a kick to the bollocks.

"Sheisse! Okay, enough, I'm sorry". The Rus…Ger…Norman said, wincing, in agony.

"That's better" Robin said, "we wouldn't want to go up a gear from the hammer now do we old chap?".

"Our plan is to take you as our guide" Brex said, "you are going to lead us right to your king".

"Um, when did we decide this?" Boudicca asked.

"Yes, if your plan was to get me to lead you to my king, then it was probably a good move to smash my toes into tiny bits so I can hardly walk".

Brex punched him hard in the face again.

"Listen my dear boy" Arthur said, casually tossing a large knife into the air and catching it again "if we want you to lead us there, you WILL lead us there, and you will crawl if need be. We are going to kill your king, and you are going to be the one who takes us to him".

The Norman looked at his bloody foot and shook his head slowly, his shoulders slumped defeatedly.

"Sheisse".

"Cut".

Percival insisted that they had another go at the scene, demanding that this time Big Stevie sticks one hundred percent to the script, and then they had a break while the next scene was set up.

"So, you're a woman then, technically", Big Stevie said to the actress playing Boudicca, who he hadn't bothered learning the name of. "Does it feel weird that you have equal billing with the rest of us? You know, considering that we can ACTUALLY fight. Well, I can at least, but even these limp-wristed little boys will be tougher than a woman".

"Excuse me? I'm a black belt in four different martial arts and I spent ten years in the army, fighting all over the world while you were playing at being a hardman in crappy films. I think I can safely say that I'm the equal of any of you".

He chuckled.

"Bless. Look, I'm sure you're pretty tough, for a woman, but real fighting is for men like me, and I think that people are going to have a hard time believing in your character. I did suggest that it would be more realistic to make you my love interest, along to keep me satisfied in the periods when my character isn't kicking ass, but the amateurs in charge thought that they knew better".

"I don't think that would have been very believable Stephen, for one thing I'm half your age".

The Unbearable Heaviness of Stephen Seagull.

"Oh come on you're older than twenty, and I don't look my age".

She laughed. "Stephen, you've been forty for about twenty years now, isn't it about time to admit your real age? You're old enough to be my grandad, and for the record I'm thirty-two".

"How dare you! I'm in my early forties, and look and fight like it too. The only thing about me that is old is my blues soul when I sing and play my guitar".

"I've heard your music and it does indeed sound like the work of as very old man, with crippling arthritis in his fingers. Anyway Stephen as much as I have enjoyed our chat I have to go a bit further away from you and stare at that tree. Bye".

She walked away, Big Stevie shrugged, and walked over to "Arthur", roundhouse kicking a stuntman on the way.

Arthur was leaning against a tree smoking a fag, and smiled when Big Stevie approached.

"Oh hello Stephen, we didn't get a chance to talk before, it's nice to meet you".

"I know it is. So I see that Boudicca chick is a lesbian eh, makes sense".

"Oh, I didn't know, not that it matters. She's been doing well though, considering she doesn't have much acting experience. I'm hoping this will get me a foot in the door to Hollywood, I've always fancied trying to make it over there".

"Hollywood isn't all it's cracked up to be Arthur, they are a bit behind the times and don't really know much about proper art. Still, a mediocre actor like you would probably fit right in".

"Thanks...My name is Paul by the way".

"Ah, if it's okay with you I'll just keep calling you Arthur, I get confused on film sets trying to remember which name is the characters' and which name is the actor's one so no offence, but I'll stick to Arthur, Paul Bytheway".

"No problem Stephen; sorry, Brex", Paul laughed, which wasn't reciprocated.

"Can I ask you something about this film Arthur? When I looked through the script it looked like we lose in the end, but that can't be right. What is the point of a film where the heroes lose?"

"No Stephen, that is exactly what happens as this is based on a true story, and the Normans did in fact succeed in their invasion. We have just added a little sub-plot to history in a what-if? manner, but we can't exactly change real life".

"Maybe if your king had gotten a few more American mercenaries over rather than just the one then the Normans wouldn't have won. I just don't know if all my fans are going to accept me being on the losing side".

"Oh don't worry Stephen it's a noble defeat, and we get very close to succeeding. Plus your death is incredibly emotional, assuming your acting is up to it of course".

"I DIE?"

39

The Unbearable Heaviness of Stephen Seagull.

"Yes, I thought you said you'd read the script?"

"Well to be honest I did what I usually do, skim read the whole thing to see how many fight scenes I win, and have a quick scan for any sexy time with a young babe. How on earth can you expect to kill STEPHEN SEAGULL and not create a massive worldwide uproar?"

"Stephen, this is a shitty little independent British film, whose audience will probably consist of my mum and her cat, so I think it's safe to say there isn't going to be any massive uproar at the ending. Come on Stephen, just think of the money and don't take it all too seriously; it's not Citizen Kane".

"I don't give a shit about Shakespeare! This is the action genre, which is supposed to be taken very seriously indeed, and the fans just won't accept a legendary figure like me dying; it just isn't realistic".

"Well you can take it up with Percival then" Arthur sighed, as Percival beckoned them back to action.

"Don't worry, I will".

"Okay", said Percival, gathering them round, "in this scene Brex is dying after the failed assassination attempt, and the rest of you are comforting him. Well, apart from you extras who will have died previously, you can bugger off for a shower".

"Wait, I'm already dead in this scene? I wanted to talk to you about that" Big Stevie said, confused.

"Stephen, you must know with all your experience in film that sometimes scenes are filmed out of sequence? Anyway, what did you want to talk about?"

"I just think that my character shouldn't die, and in fact he should be the one who kills William".

"Stephen, William doesn't die, he can't! We would be re-writing history! This is a very serious production, and historical accuracy is very important to me if I want to be taken seriously as a director. I'm sorry, but the story remains as it is. Now let's crack on and get this scene done".

"Action".

Robin sat on a hillside, quietly humming the American national anthem as he played a lute, head bowed. Brex lay at his feet, mortally wounded, with Arthur and Boudicca kneeling down on either side.

"G...getting cold..." Brex stammered, clutching his bleeding side.

Arthur gently laid his anorak over his comrade, and fluffed his pillow.

"It's okay Brex" Boudicca soothed, a solitary tear falling down her cheek, "soon you will be in Valhalla fighting alongside all the other gods and heroes: Thor, Odin, Zeus, that one with the trident, Jupiter, Spock and the rest. You are going to a better place, a place fit for a warrior such as yourself".

"Yes old friend" Arthur said, placing a hand on Brex's shoulder lovingly, "while we are down here in the shit and the mud you will be up there getting drunk with nubile young women and fighting to your heart's content. We will miss you though, old boy". He looked away, embarrassed by the tears welling in his eyes.

The Unbearable Heaviness of Stephen Seagull.

"Th...thank you Arthur...and you too Boudicca...I...see a...light in the...distance" he raised a faltering hand, pointing into the night. His friends looked, but could see nothing except for a horse having a shit behind a wagon.

Robin had finished the anthem, and slowly began to sing Amazing Grace, his voice trembling and cracking with emotion.

"M...make me...a promise" Brex spluttered, blood now running from his mouth.

"Anything Brex" Boudicca sobbed.

"Make sure you...kill that...commie bastard...stone-cold dead for me...will...ya?"

Boudicca gently kissed his cheek.

"You have our word Brex, you have our word".

"The...light...is...getting...brighter, I see...a...golden...chariot...pulled...by...winged...white...horses..."

"It's okay Brex, go now" Arthur whispered, clasping his friend's hands in his own, "go to Valhalla".

Robin threw down the lute and walked quickly away , his shoulders heaving and the unmistakable sound of weeping coming from him. Boudicca got up and went after him, embracing him as they stood together in the moonlight, comforting each other as they wept.

"Go friend" Arthur said, and pulled the anorak slowly up over his now silent comrade's face. He looked in the direction his friend had pointed, and wept silently.

"Aaaaaaaaaaaaand cut!"

Tough crew members stood around, unashamedly crying, and a few burst into spontaneous applause at the incredibly powerful scene they had just witnessed. Boudicca, Arthur and Robin continued crying for real, shaken with the pure emotion of it all, and Percival ran towards them all, smiling broadly despite his tears.

"That was amazing everybody, tremendous work! My god Stephen, that was some of the best acting I've ever seen! I can smell an Oscar coming and no mistake! I really don't know how we..." he halted for a second, puzzled by the strange noise he was hearing, but then realised that it was Big Stevie snoring loudly under the anorak.

"I think we'll have a break now people for lunch, so everyone can compose themselves again".

The cast and crew walked away to catering in quiet contemplation, the only sound in the night Big Stevie's loud snoring, occasionally punctuated by a loud, elongated sleep-fart.

The Unbearable Heaviness of Stephen Seagull.

The film wrapped up four weeks later, and everyone was excited about its prospects. Big Stevie did a lot of promotion for the film, doing the rounds of every chat show that couldn't afford a decent guest. The film managed to get a limited release in the cinemas, but unfortunately it didn't quite take off as they had hoped, and things went quiet on the offers front again. Big Stevie knew that the money from the film wasn't going to keep him in rented underpants forever, so decided it was time to write another script himself. Wonky-legs MacGuffin was about a former special forces commander who had lost the use of his legs saving a little girl from a rhino stampede in one of the countries where rhinos live, and was now wheelchair-bound. Big Stevie thought that this was a masterstroke, as it meant that he didn't have to get up off his arse for the whole film. Wonky-legs MacGuffin now worked as a private investigator, and in the film he was on a case where a young girl had gone missing from her school amid suspicious circumstances. The film was going to be an epic, which would include the Italian mafia, the KKK, the Russian mafia (well duh!), some posh English baddies, some noble Native Americans, the Yakuza, the Triads, some shifty looking chavs in a Fiat, and Mexican drug cartels.

Unfortunately Punchy Ponytail Productions had long since gone into liquidation as people kept forgetting to watch any of their films, so Big Stevie would have to get the money necessary from elsewhere. He could have gone to one of the huge Hollywood companies and got the money from them of course, they wouldn't have given their right arm for a new Stephen Seagull film, absolutely no doubt about that, but he decided that he would like to give a smaller independent company a chance instead. He put his agent on the case and a mere nine months later they had a company all lined up: Donald's Taxi and Film Company Ltd., a small, but ambitious film company that operated from the office of a taxi firm in London. It would mean going back to the UK, but Big Stevie was confident that he could navigate his way around the city now, and had gotten used to their quaint old-timey ways.

"Going to London, see you in eight weeks time". He shouted to Susan as he went out the front door a few days later. He locked her in, and got in the taxi to head to the airport. He had decided against taking her with him this time as it would save money, and he was confident that the hotel cleaners would be able to keep his room to an acceptable level of hygiene without her help. She was a nice enough woman, probably, with soft, pliant hands and reasonable cooking skills, but he wasn't going to be able to drag a sexy young extra back to his hotel room if she was already locked up in there. No, it was better (and cheaper) if she stayed at home with the vacuum cleaner, lawnmower, power-washer, washing machine and cement mixer.

Once he landed back in London he booked into a different hotel from the last time, and then went to meet Donald at his cab firm office.

"Hello Donald, may I sit" Big Stevie panted, mopping the sweat from his brow. It had been quite a walk from the cab parked right outside the door to the office inside.

"Sure big fella, you can rest yer old plates of meat over there, cor blimey".

Big Stevie slumped into the chair, and pulled a Twix from his pocket to keep his blood sugar levels up.

"I must say it's an honour to 'ave such an esteemed action star in my little old cab office, Gawd bless our queen and so on." Donald was a chubby little avuncular chap, a small cigar hanging from his lips.

"So you've read my script?"

The Unbearable Heaviness of Stephen Seagull.

"Sure OI 'ave, apples n' pears, roll out the barrel. Oi must say it's one of the best scripts I've ever read in my life, and I've read over seven of them".

Big Stevie chuckled confidently, "I knew you would, it's certainly the best script I've ever read. So, I presume that the budget is all in place and we're good to go?"

Donald shuffled awkwardly in his seat, and looked out of the window.

"Almost Stephen, I've got six cabs out on quite long fares at the moment so hopefully the money they take back will get us up to our budget, give or take…"

"Can I ask how many films your company has made? It's just that I borrowed someone's computer and went on the internet and I couldn't find anything listed for your company online".

"Er…well…truth be told me ol' China this will be the first, but first of many I can guarantee you that. Snooker Loopy. The company has admittedly been 99.999999% cab firm and 0.000001% film so far, but that's all gonna change soon, and with you in our first feature we can't possibly fail, can we?"

"Failure is not a word in my vocabluleralily, this film WILL be a success with me at the helm, mark my words".

"Great stuff treacle! Cor blimey we're gonna have some fun together n' no mistake! Now, come through the back and meet the rest of the cast. The Krays nevva 'urt their own".

Big Stevie sighed. It felt like he'd only just sat down, but with a grunt he heaved himself out of the seat and followed Donald through into a tumbleweed-strewn alleyway, even though Big Stevie was pretty sure that tumbleweed wasn't actually a thing in London. There stood seven men and one token woman, idly watching a couple of cats humping on a wall.

"Stephen" Donald said, walked over to one of the men and slapping him cordially on the shoulder, "this is Gary Steptoe, one of your co-stars in the film. We predict great things for this lad after his stunning performance as a postie over three episodes in a well-respected soap over 'ere called Hollyoaks".

"Hi Stephen, great to meet you" Gary said, offering a hand.

Big Stevie ignored the hand, and looked Gary up and down slowly.

"Looks like I'll be the alpha on this set yet again" he sneered. He looked around at the rest of the cast, shaking his head and sighing loudly.

"Don't bother introducing me to these other losers" He said to Donald, as he turned and walked away, "just tell them to do their job and stay out of my way".

As he strode slowly back to the door leading to the office he knew that they would be impressed by this take-no-shit, incredibly masculine display of dominance, and hoped that the large, dark, sweat patch running down the crack of the arse of his jeans wasn't TOO visible to them.

The Unbearable Heaviness of Stephen Seagull.

Day one on the set of the film, Master of Warriors, and they were sitting in a pub owned by a mate of Donald. It was a quiet Tuesday afternoon, and they hadn't bothered to close the pub as there was only one pishy old bloke sleeping against the bar anyway, and he would save them having to pay for an extra. Big Stevie, sitting at a table in his wheelchair across from two shady-looking types, was undercover and about to discuss a black-market deal. They were waiting patiently for the director to turn up, a man (SURELY) that Big Stevie hadn't met yet.

"Alright lads, let's get started!" shouted Donald as he came crashing through the door, holding a megaphone.

"When does the director get here?" Big Stevie asked, wheeling around from the table.

"I AM the director Stephen; Chas n' Dave, jellied eels n' whatnot".

"What? Have you ever directed a film before?"

"Nah, but how hard can it be? In a way I direct my cabbies all day anyway, so I'll just imagine that you're all cabbies and Bob's your Auntie's live-in lover".

"Wait a minute" Big Stevie protested angrily, "I'm a hugely-respected actor, held in high regard worldwide".

A few murmurs rumbled around the room.

"I've worked for some of the best directors a small amount of money can buy", he continued. "and you expect me to listen to a taxi firm owner?"

"Now Stephen, don't get yourself worked up me old mucker, you're here now so you may as well crack on with it, especially as you've signed the contract and already taken your fee out of my account".

Big Stevie simmered for a moment, but eventually turned back towards the table.

"Well let's get on with it then, I can probably help you along as we go, as I basically direct most of the films I've worked on anyway".

"Fantastic! Right, let's crack on then...ACTION!"

"So Mr. Smith, have you brought the money?"

"I have" said Big Stevie, John Smith being his character's undercover alias.

"Let's see it then" said the second man.

"First things first, let me see the merchandise".

The two men looked at each other, but eventually the first one took out a briefcase and opened it on the table, being careful to shield the contents from the barmaid and the sleeping old pishy man.

"John" nodded approvingly.

"Looks good, very good indeed".

The Unbearable Heaviness of Stephen Seagull.

"Okay, now it is your turn, let's see the money".

"John" bent down with a bit of effort and pulled his own briefcase up from under the table.

"Here you go lads".

He opened the briefcase on the table slightly, and one of the men leaned in closer. Suddenly "John" opened it fully and a large boxing glove on a spring shot out of the briefcase, hitting the man right on the nose with a loud BOING! and knocking him out straightaway, believably. The other man sprang into action, pulling a gun, but Wonky-legs had spun towards him in his chair and crashed into him, sending the gun flying. The man threw a couple of punches at Wonky-legs, which the fat ageing man in a wheelchair easily avoided, and Wonky-legs waved his hands in front of his face slowly, in a manner that to the untrained eye would have done the square root of fuck all to such a large, powerful young thug, but in fact, somehow, knocked the young man crashing to the floor, knocked out.

Wonky-legs turned to the attractive young barmaid and smiled.

"Sorry darling, I appear to have spilt my drink".

The young woman burst out laughing and gave him a sensual, lingering look, as she found this stranger not only sexy, charismatic, and potent, despite him being a clinically-obese older bloke with piggy-eyes and a clearly badly-dyed goatee and ponytail, but hilariously funny too.

"Cut".

Donald rushed into the centre of the pub, a huge grin all over his face. "People, that was fantastic! Everyone was spot on, well done! Hopefully we managed to capture it all on camera beautifully, I told you all this directing would be a piece of piss!"

The barmaid stepped forward, "Camera?"

"Yeah, camera! You know, those massive things over there in the...shit. Take a break people, I forgot to get any cameras...sorry about that, won't be long".

"It might also be an idea to get some lighting, boom-mics, and all the rest of the things you need to, you know, make a film". Big Stevie sighed.

"I've said I'm sorry! Knees up muvva Brown etc."

Donald disappeared out of the pub, leaving the cast to amuse themselves playing the bandit and getting drunk. Big Stevie's body was a temple and he didn't normally drink, but after exhausting all of his acting skills to accurately play someone who sits on his arse all day he was worn out, and pissed-off that it had all been for nothing, so decided to join the other two actors for a beer. Big Stevie was far too hard and in control to get drunk, by sheer willpower he would remain sober, so figured that there was no harm in having one or two while they waited.

"You look familiar" he said to one of the thugs, as he took a sip of his beer. "Have we met before?"

"Yes, I played one of the mercenaries who always stood in the background saying nothing on your film Lobster Claw and the Cuttlefish Platoon, I died in scene three of a punctured anus, remember?"

The Unbearable Heaviness of Stephen Seagull.

"Oh yeah, I remember you, Simon wasn't it, Simon Arkwright?"

"Peter Jamieson. Those were the days eh? The budget on that was certainly a bit bigger than on this that's for sure, Donald asked me to wear my own clothes while filming, and in the car chase later in the film he's going to take the money for the petrol I use out of my final fee, so hopefully I can nail it in a couple of takes".

"That's terrible, maybe you can get the stuntman to chip in half?"

"I doubt it, that's him over there" Peter said, pointing at the pishy old man slumped against the bar.

"I've got a horrible feeling that this film isn't going to go down in the annals as one of the greats of world cinema" the second thug said, as he put a second round of drinks onto the table.

"I just hope that it doesn't end up being filmed on Donald's phone" Peter said.

"Does anyone have any idea jush how long he ish going to be?" Big Stevie said. His mouth felt strange, but he knew that he wasn't drunk; he'd only had one pint, and no goddamn beer was gonna kick HIS ass!

"He muttered something about going to see Dodgy Dave the Fence, who can apparently get anything you want for a very reasonable price, no questions asked".

"What the hell have I got myself into?" Big Stevie mumbled, almost to himself.

"I suppose we'll make a little bit of money, regardless" Peter smiled, trying to inject a bit of hope into proceedings.

"I'm Frank by the way" the second thug said.

"Hey, I might have worked with a relative of yours, I'm shure I worked with shomeone a while ago called Arthur Bytheway, or Paul Bytheway, or something like that. Do you have any relations that are also actors?"

"Um, my name isn't…oh never mind; no, I don't think so. Anyway, do you think you will continue to act in action films for much longer Stephen? No offence but it's a young man's game, and you're knocking on a bit now. Do you think you will move into a different sphere of acting maybe?"

"What do you mean? I'm still as fit as a butcher's dog".

"My butcher's dog has got gout and a dodgy hip" Peter interjected.

"Well I'm ash fit as a marine's dog then, one that goesh to boot camp with him and does all the taining, training and every…everything. I'll be kicking ass for a long time yet guys, this body is a coiled shpring with the energy of a man half my age, which is nineteen. Now excuse me, could one of you push me through to the toilet?"

"Er, you do remember that you're not ACTUALLY disabled, don't you Stephen?"

"Of course! I was…joking". He heaved himself out of the chair and wobbled unsteadily towards the toilet. This pub seemed to have a really weird, springy carpet that made walking in a straight line really hard, but he made it to the toilet eventually. To the untrained eye it may look like he was drunk on two

The Unbearable Heaviness of Stephen Seagull.

pints, but he knew it wasn't that; he'd had a plate of fried chicken three weeks ago and he now realised that it must not have been cooked properly, and that was what was making him dizzy, a bit nauseous, and unsteady on his feet. He went into a cubicle and sat down for a bit with his eyes closed, trying to focus.

"Stephen? Stephen, are you okay?"

"Huh...what?"

"It's Peter, are you okay? It's just that you've been in there for about half an hour".

He felt drool running down his chin, and realised that he must have somehow fallen asleep, despite not being drunk at all.

"I'm okay Peter, I was jusht...meditating, I realised I'd forgotten to do it this morning and it ish an important part of my daily routine, and I thought it would be nice and quiet in here. I'm finished now though, and I'll be out in a minute".

"Okay fine, we've got another round in plus a couple of whisky chasers, so crack on and get out here for some more drinking. Donald phoned and said filming is off for the day so we may as well have some fun".

Big Stevie, got up with a bit of effort, steadied himself against the walls of the cubicle, and walked out. He washed his hands and splashed cold water onto his face in an effort to refresh himself, and then walked back to the two men, using every ounce of his incredible willpower to focus and walk straight.

"He IS alive" Frank laughed, pushing the chaser towards Big Stevie.

"Sorry, I should have meditated before I left, I'll make sure I do tomorrow".

"We thought you must be doing the world's largest non-blue whale related shit" Peter teased.

"Drink up then!"

Big Stevie forced the whisky down his throat, gagging, and quickly took a large gulp of the beer to try and get the taste out of his mouth. He could feel bile rising in his throat, and really cursed that fried chicken.

"Come on then Stephen" Frank said, pointing to his own quarter full pint glass, "You've fallen behind".

Big Stevie gulped two large glugs of beer down, and felt the room beginning to spin.

"Anyone fancy some crisps?" He said, hoping something to eat would quell his queasy stomach.

"Yeah great idea Stephen, it's your round anyway so get some drinks while you're up there" Frank said, gulping down the last of his beer.

Big Stevie groaned inwardly, and pushed his protesting body back out of the comfy wheelchair. He had JUST sat down, but thought he'd better not go to the bar in the wheelchair after the comment last time. He ordered three more beers, three more chasers (after a shout to that end from Peter), and six packets of crisps, hoping that four should be enough for him to ease his dodgy guts.

The Unbearable Heaviness of Stephen Seagull.

"So Stephen" Frank said, as Big Stevie flopped down into the wheelchair again. "What are you doing working for such an amateurish company as this? I thought you could do better".

"Well, I think it's important to encourage new people into the industry, and give something back. I must admit that I didn't realise quite what the set up was here though, or I might definitely have thought twice".

This was bollocks as Donald's offer was literally the only one he'd got, but no need to tell them this.

"So then, come on, tell us who you would least like to fight out of all the other screen tough guys" Peter said.

"Huh" Big Stevie snorted, spraying crisps over the table. "There are no other screen tough guysh, only wannabes."

"Ah come on" Frank chided, "What about Jean Claude Van Damme?"

"Pfft, I offered to step outside with him once at a party and he shobered up incredibly sharply, once he realised that this was REAL life, and I wasn't going to go down like so many of the actors paid to do so on his crappy films".

"Dolph?"

"Dolphins would scare me more".

"Sly?"

"Oh come on! Those three together wouldn't dare to take me on! I'm the only real deal in Hollywood, the rest of them are just actors, pretending to be hard".

"So is there no-one at all in the world of film you wouldn't like to fight, absolutely no-one?" Peter asked.

"Well okay, I will concede that there is ONE possible person I wouldn't go out of my way to fight, and that's Robocop".

"Peter Weller?" Frank asked, a touch surprised. "Wouldn't he be in his seventies by now?"

"Who? Who the hell is Peter Weller? I'm talking about Robocop, that half-man half-machine cop from the film, I think he would give me quite a fight before I inevitably managed to overpower him. I can't see it happening though, he seemed to shun the limelight after those films he did back then so I probably wouldn't be able to find him to challenge him even if I wanted to. His fighting skills might be a bit rusty, literally!" Big Stevie burst into raucous laughter at his clever joke, which proved he could be witty, as well as being a hard, handsome, muscular polymath.

"Um, Stephen" Frank said, looking slightly embarrassed, "You do know that he was a character, don't you?"

"Really? He never sheemed like much of a chalac...character in those films, in fact he seemed pretty straight-laced, humourless and by-the-book to me. I mean to a certain extent I understand, as he was under a lot of pressure upholding the law, but he could have lightened up a little. I tell you what though,

The Unbearable Heaviness of Stephen Seagull.

we could do with more Robocops on our lawless streets nowadays, I've no idea why the government discontinued the idea".

"It was probably a cost thing…"Peter said, rolling his eyes at Frank, who was returning with another round.

Big Stevie felt the urge to have another piss, but tried to ignore it. He was beginning to feel very unwell now, and really wished that the filming hadn't been paused.

"Are you married Stephen?"

"Yeah, to a woman called…um…it's on the tip of my tongue…Susan! That's it! Lovely woman, probably. she's from Colombia or somewhere".

"Kids?"

"No, I don't think the world deserves more of my DNA in it, we would overpower you all with our potency. Are you two married? kids?" Big Stevie asked out of politeness, not really giving a flying fuck about their personal lives.

"I'm split up from my wife, and have two sons and a daughter" Frank said.

"Married with a son" Peter said.

"What did you think of the script" Big Stevie asked, keen to return to his favourite subject: himself. "Fantastic, isn't it?".

There was a brief moment of silence.

"It has some great…fight scenes Stephen" Frank said eventually.

"It's great how I manage to get all the major crime gangs to all get together for a great big fight isn't it?"

"Yes" Peter replied, "it was totally believable and in no way contrived".

"I do have a question though Stephen" Frank said, "you know that scene where you beat up eight Yakuza hitmen? Do you think that will realistic considering that you are in a wheelchair?"

"Of course! I'm not just any old man in a wheelchair, I'm Stephen Seagull! People will totally buy that I could do it".

There was another moments silence.

"Also, another thing, I just wonder if in todays more enlightened times whether it is a good idea to have Wonky-legs' twenty-year-old nurse falling for him. Wouldn't it be better to have the woman nearer his own age and then it might be a nice little sub-plot, rather than looking a little seedy?"

"Seedy? Why on earth would it be seedy for a slightly younger woman to fall for a sexy older man, still in his absolute physical prime, rather than one of those wet liberal weaklings of her own age? She showers me every day, of course she's going to get shexulal feelings!"

"Yeah and she wipes your arse every day too" Frank laughed, "which is probably a bit less of a turn on…"
99

The Unbearable Heaviness of Stephen Seagull.

"I think you guys are just a little bit jealous that I can pull a twenty-year old gorgeous nurse and you couldn't".

"Yes, in a film script, which you wrote yourself".

"No, there is definitely the touch of the green-eyed mon..."suddenly a fountain of vomit spewed from Big Stevie's mouth, plastering the table and most of Frank's torso. Another blast of food followed a few seconds later, filling their pint glasses on the table and dripping down onto the floor.

Frank and Peter shot up from their seats in disgust, as the barmaid stifled a laugh.

"Sorry lads, I had a fried chicken three we..." another rush of partially-digested food came spewing out of his mouth, all over the carpet where he sat. He slumped forward and slithered down onto the floor, cradling himself in a foetal position, whimpering slightly. Frank was already in the toilet cleaning himself up, and Peter was at the bar apologising to the barmaid.

"Peter...Peter..." Big Stevie said weakly, shivering and feeling his stomach growling unsettling again. "Could you help me up into my chair Peter and push me home?".

The Unbearable Heaviness of Stephen Seagull.

Filming had to be cancelled the next day as A) Donald still hadn't quite managed to obtain all of the necessary equipment needed to make a film, and B) The lead actor and um...main draw was ill in bed all day with an allergic reaction to um, fried chicken. Finally on the third day everything was good to go, though Big Stevie was still feeling a little bit groggy, but he manfully loaded up on painkillers and copious bottles of water. They got the pub scene out of the way and then moved onto Donald's flat, which was going to be used as the home of the boss of the Yakuza.

"Right, in this scene Stephen you, as John Smith, are trying to set the Yakuza against the chavs in the Fiat, in the hope that one will eliminate the other".

"Yes, I know, I wrote the scene".

"Fair enough pilchard, let's crack on then...ACTION!"

"Er, Donald" an actor playing a Yakuza henchman said, "sorry, but are we not going to change any of the décor?"

"What for?"

"Well, I mean it's not impossible, but are many high-ranking Japanese criminal masterminds massive fans of Minder for example?" The henchman asked, pointing to a poster of Terry n' Arthur from the eighties classic TV programme blue-tacked to the wall.

"Oh come on, no-one's gonna be looking at the background, they'll be captivated by the powerhouse acting from these two fine gentlemen. Gercha!"

"Well, it's not just that, I mean you have a lovely home Donald but it's a bit um, cosy for a multi-millionaire. Would a big Yakuza boss REALLY live in a tiny little flat with a bed that pulls out from the wall, and the only cooking appliance is a George Foreman grill?"

"Now that we're talking about this" the actor playing the main boss interjected, "I do wonder if the George and Mildred curtains should maybe be taken down?"

"And who exactly are Cannon and Ball?" Big Stevie asked, pointing to another poster on the wall.

"Stephen! You philistine! Next you'll be telling me you don't know who Jim Bowen is!" Donald said, pointing to the massive Bullseye painting covering the entire back wall.

"Also" Big Stevie continued, "I don't want to look like we're picking holes in your lovely home, and I know that many rich people go for the spartan, less-is-more approach to home furnishings, but I still think he would have more furniture in his main room than two deckchairs and what looks like a bird table".

"It will all look fine on film boys, I swear. We'll just turn the lights down low and have everyone standing, except for Wonky-legs of course. Give us a hand to shift the deckchairs and bird table out into the garden will ya?"

They cleared the room, closed the George and Mildred curtains, and turned the lights down very low.

"Okay, action!"

101

The Unbearable Heaviness of Stephen Seagull.

"So Mr Miyagi that concludes our deal, and I thank you for your time. There's just one more thing I'd like to talk to you about, and that's the Cleethorpes Bludz."

"Who?"

"The Cleethorpes Bludz, a rival gang who have been encroaching onto your territory and saying disrespectful things about you all".

"Sorry John but I've never heard of them, and if they were any kind of threat then I would have".

"Oh believe me, they're a threat all right, one I think you should squash as soon as you can".

"Are they a big gang? I just think I'd have heard of them if they were serious contenders".

"Well, there are only five of them squashed into a little Fiat, but they do a disproportionate amount of damage for their size, especially to your reputation and operation".

"Let me make a call".

Mr. Miyagi fumbled around in the darkness for a phone, landing in Wonky-legs' lap at one point. Eventually he found it and went through to another room. Well actually he walked into a cupboard, but as it was dark and the camera couldn't see anything properly anyway he shut the door behind him and squashed in beside the vacuums, coats, boots, and various other items of clothing and junk, and proceeded to mutter quietly on the phone. After a few minutes he came back out, being careful to slide out of a small gap in the door so the camera didn't see anything.

"John, you need not worry yourself any longer about the Cleethorpes Bludz, I have tasked my main man to hunt them down and eliminate them".

"Good call Mr. Miyagi".

"Well if that concludes our business?"

"Yes, thank you. Now, I'd best go and talk to my other associates, until next time".

"Bye John".

Wonky-legs turned his wheelchair and went to the door, knocking over an On the Buses framed picture as he wheeled around in the gloom, and bashing his knees on the front door.

"Cut".

"That went great" Big Stevie said, rubbing his knees in the wheelchair.

"Fantastic!" Donald agreed, "luvly jubbly!".

"Right everyone, let's go to the car park and shoot the big fight scene" the cinematographer (Donald's mum, not having a fucking clue what a cinematographer is or does, but she does make a lovely cup of tea. Sorry, Rosie Lee) said.

The car park was just over a mile away and some of it was uphill, so Peter was pretty knackered after pushing Big Stevie all the way there in the wheelchair. Big Stevie claimed it was because he was going all
102

The Unbearable Heaviness of Stephen Seagull.

method and staying in character at all times rather than just being a lazy cunt, but it had been noted that this was forgotten every time he jumped out of the chair to run to the ice cream van that came round Donald's street every night.

Big Stevie got into position in the car park as three Russian thugs, two Triads, Brian the only remaining by this stage chav, and two Mexican cartel members surrounded him menacingly.

"Action".

"So now we know who you really are Mr. Smith" one of the Russians said, taking out a large knife, "Or should I say, Wonky-legs MacGuffin! Unfortunately there are going to be two deaths today, Wonky-legs MacGuffin and John Smith".

"Give it your best shot tough guy", Wonky-legs growled.

All eight thugs pounced, but Wonky-legs waved his hands in front of him as they neared and these masterful martial arts moves knocked every one of them flying, somehow. Despite Wonky-legs chair being rooted to the spot and Wonky-legs moving his hands about three inches half-heartedly, both Russians lay dead, one of the Triads lay stunned on the ground with two broken legs and a punctured lung, the other was running away into the distance crying, the two Mexicans were on their hands and knees coughing up blood, and Brian the chav was hanging upside down from the top of a lamppost, dazed.

"Come back when you're big enough" Wonky-legs wheezed to the wounded Triad, dripping sweat onto him from his beetroot-red face. He took a gun out of his pocket and pointed it at the prone Chinese man.

"Now, where is the girl?"

"Cut".

Another scene in the bag, and the film was already looking like a future classic. Filming was finished for the day as most of the cast had to start their shifts in the taxi firm, so Big Stevie thought he may as well go for a chippy and eat it down by the river. He was sitting in the pleasant evening sun eating his double cheeseburger and chips when a group of young men in their early twenties approached him.

"Give us a chip chubs", a lank-haired skinny one at the front said.

"And give us one of those burgers too, you've had enough for one life by the look of you" a short bloke shouted, not exactly skinny himself.

"Piss off and get your own".

"OOOoooo, get him" the first bloke laughed, as the others taunted and laughed at Big Stevie in the background. "Whatcha gonna do, run us over?"

"You think I need this wheelchair to kick all of your asses? If I start on you all then you are entering a world of pain".

The Unbearable Heaviness of Stephen Seagull.

"Ha ha! You couldn't beat an egg ya fat shite! So give us the rest of your chips and we won't puncture your tyres".

"Ok, on your own heads be it". Big Stevie got up out of the wheelchair (after three attempts), laid down his chips, took off his jacket, and picked up his chips again.

"Anyone wants a chip they have to fight me for it".

"Fine by us" a stocky bloke said, approaching Big Stevie menacingly. The other seven followed behind, and Big Stevie suddenly regretted getting out of the chair. It was going to be hard to fight eight young men, especially while trying not to drop his chips.

"This reminds me of one of my films", he said in a sudden burst of inspiration.

"Fuck off, you're not in films!"

"Oh no? maybe you've heard of a little film called Death Walrus?"

"Nope, sounds shit".

"It's BRILLIANT. Okay, how about Hammerteeth?"

"Sounds shit too".

"Military Mercenaries?"

"Bloodbaths and Bloodshowers?"

"Deathkiller?"

"Axe Warrior?"

"Middle-East Beast?"

"Blade of the Gun?"

"Suck My Bazooka?"

"Kicked to Fatality?"

"Grizzly McAllister?"

(14 minutes later).

"Skull Attack?"

"Cowboys and Injuries?"

"Moscow Mayhem?"

"Hyper Sniper?"

"Blood of the Banshee?"

The Unbearable Heaviness of Stephen Seagull.

"Trapped on a big Ship?"

"Trapped on a Big Ship! Yeah, I've seen that! Were you in that?"

"I was the main man".

"Nah, he wasn't an obese, sweaty oaf with a face so big and red Martian invaders would use you as a second home".

"No, that was me! Just a little younger, that's all".

"And a little littler too, that was a good few chip suppers ago that one!"

"Don't you recognise my ponytail?"

"So did you pork the lass with the huge jugs?"

Big Stevie grinned "well what do you think?"

"Probably not, she was tidy as fuck and you look like someone has put an XXXX size tracksuit onto a blancmange, and then Gene Simmons stood over it and shaved his pubes".

"Well I did! She was begging for a proper relationship after a night with me, but I was happy playing the field, as a sexy young famous actor".

"You were pretty tough in that film, all those years ago".

"That's my genre, I do action films, on account of being a black belt in various martial arts and general fighting expert. Even films I'm not actually in or have written I'm called to assist in making the fight scenes realistic".

"Who is the toughest now then, on film?"

"Ha, on film most of them are tough but none of them are actually tough in real life, and would have been destroyed in any of the dojos I taught in, never mind in any of the war zones I've been in".

"You fought in real life? Have you killed anyone?"

"You name a conflict from World War Two to the present day that America has been involved in officially or unofficially and I've fought in it, sometimes changing the outcome of the whole thing; off the record of course".

"But have you killed anyone?"

"Let's just say that I'm trained in every weapon you can think of from long-range missiles to close-quarters combat and I've used all of these weapons hundreds, if not thousands of times, so I'm sure you can figure it out", Big Stevie winked, sitting back down into the chair to ease his struggling legs.

"So is that why you have the wheelchair, did you get injured fighting?"

"No actually, it's from when I saved my comrade Bronnigan "Fists of Mayhem" Corpsegrinder from an attack by seven machete-wielding madmen in Sierra Leone. I had killed six of them but the seventh

The Unbearable Heaviness of Stephen Seagull.

managed to get a lucky blow in, his machete going right through the base of my spine, severing it. The field doctors were amazed that I had managed to crawl over two miles through jungle terrain in that state, and not only that, but with my wounded colleague Bronnigan on my back. Once I was flown home the medical experts said that there was no chance I would ever walk again, it was a physical impossibility, but they weren't dealing with a normal man and in just three weeks I was hobbling down the hospital ward unaided, and in another five I ran another New York marathon, finishing a slow for me but admirable under the circumstances seventh".

"But if you were up and about running marathons so quickly, how come you need a wheelchair to get about now?"

"Um…er…yes well my problem the doctors said was that I was too tough for my own good, and although my bones, muscle, heart etc. are approximately 73% stronger than a normal man's, I had still put them under too much pressure too quickly, and my body relapsed. Now I have to use the chair for a year until my body has recovered. Of course being the man I am I occasionally forget and get out of the chair, especially if I get the chance to fight, which I love and I'm still great at, but then I remember that the doctor said more than one minute standing and my heart will seize, and I will die".

"Ha, I think you're full of bullshit, but I find you quite entertaining" the skinny one said, laughing. "We'll let you have all your chips and…oh, you're already finished anyway. Still, we're not going to bother you anymore, enjoy staring at the river fat guy, see ya".

The group walked off, waving at Big Stevie and laughing.

"Keep your eyes peeled for Master of Warriors, my latest film!"

"Yeah, might be a laugh, all the best big fella".

They left, and Big Stevie felt good: he had displayed the art of fighting without fighting, as the great (though nowhere near as tough as Big Stevie) Bruce Lee had talked about. He knew, and they did too, that he would have destroyed them all if it had come down to a physical fight, but he had chosen the nobler way, and beat them subtly with intelligence. As he wheeled himself back to the hotel for a snack from the mini-bar, he thought about how much he had grown as a warrior from the young, brash straight-in-there-fists-swinging hardman he had been, to the older, wiser, more philosophical, but still as hard-as-nails elder statesman sat in that wheelchair he didn't need, stinking of chip-fat.

The Unbearable Heaviness of Stephen Seagull.

They were in the last week of filming, and Donald had called Big Stevie into his office.

"Come in Stevie, I've made a bit of space for you, just wheel into that corner there. Now Stevie me old China, I'm gonna cut to the chase: we're skint. Up the 'Ammers".

"What do you mean, skint?"

"It means we're brassic, out of spondoolics, not even a monkey to our name".

"No, I still don't have a clue what you are talking about Donald".

"We are completely out of money Stephen, we don't have enough to film the last scene".

"But I thought you said everything was in place, budget-wise?"

"It was Stephen, it was, but that was before you decided you weren't happy with the scene in the gardening centre and insisted on take after take after take, and I ended up having to buy sixteen fish suppers for the cast and crew as filming went on into the night, and that sent us over-budget".

"But we're almost completed! We can't finish now with the end in sight!"

"Calm down Stephen all hope isn't lost, we just need to find a way of raising a bit more money, and quickly".

"Could you put the taxi fares up a bit?"

"No, I couldn't do that, our prices already went up in March to try and raise a bit of capital to start the film side of things, and our customers would just start using Mary's Cabs down the road instead".

"I don't have any spare money, if that's what you're asking".

"No, that wasn't what I was thinking, there's this woman..."

"Yes?"

"This woman, she is very comfortably off, and is more than willing to invest the necessary cash to finish our film, and all she wants is a weekend with you after it is all over".

Big Stevie grinned. "Rich and good taste eh? Sounds like the perfect woman, I'm up for that".

"I wasn't sure whether to broach the subject with you Stephen, I know you're a married man".

"Huh? Oh, right, Susan, no, that's okay as we have an open marriage, though I'll probably have to get around to telling her that sometime soon. Look, to be honest I'm always on the lookout for an upgrade, so I would be happy to meet this woman and spend the weekend with her. I presume that she's a babe yes?".

"Well...I'm sure she was a handsome woman in her day, and she has decent feet".

"In her day? How old is she?"

"I'm not sure exactly, maybe your age, or a little bit older".

The Unbearable Heaviness of Stephen Seagull.

"MY AGE? I'm a fucking star! Why the FUCK would I be interested in a woman that old? You can forget it".

"Stephen, if you don't then the film doesn't happen, it's that simple. Do you really want all of your hard work writing the script and doing all the filming we've already done to go to waste? Come on Stephen, do it for your art; you never know, you might enjoy it".

"Can I think about it? I have an image to maintain, and if anyone was to see me in public with a woman who isn't a pneumatic blonde bombshell half my age, then people might think that I'm no longer a superstar who can have his pick of the best women, but some kind of past it, no longer relevant nobody".

"Stephen, we don't have time to think about it, we need the money now. You have to do it or we're screwed".

"She had better not be expecting me to sleep with her then".

"Cushty, I knew you would see sense. I'll tell her the good news and we can crack on with filming".

"I'd better not live to regret this".

The Unbearable Heaviness of Stephen Seagull.

With the money now secured the film was wrapped up, and the benefactor had even thrown in a bit of extra money to throw a wrap party, which was a plate of scotch eggs and a twelve pack of supermarket own brand lager for the cast and crew of twenty-three in the taxi office. Big Stevie said an emotional goodbye to everyone and wheeled out into the night, ready to order a wheelchair-accessible taxi back to the hotel.

"Stephen".

He turned round to see Donald coming quickly out of the taxi firm's door.

"Yeah Donald?"

"Two things Stephen: one, I'll need my mum's wheelchair back as she hasn't left the house in eight weeks, and two, remember you are going to be spending the weekend with Janet, and if you don't she is going to sue us for every penny both of us haven't got".

Big Stevie reluctantly got out of the wheelchair and gave it to Donald. His calves began to hurt.

"I haven't forgotten our deal Donald, I'll keep up my end of the bargain".

"See that you do Stephen, or she'll be straight on the old dog and bone to her lawyers".

"Do you think she would be willing to wear a Megan Fox mask all weekend?"

"No Stephen, I don't think she will be happy to do that. You're meeting her on Saturday morning at nine o'clock at the Tortured Squirrel hotel. She said you should wear something sexy".

"I've got a new tracksuit, it's nice and shiny".

"Okay, well good luck then, and I'll see you at the film premier. Two fer a paaahn".

Two days later Big Stevie was waiting outside the Tortured Squirrel, London's poshest hotel and a mecca for pop stars, sports stars, Russian oligarchs, internet billionaires, and Tony from Hollyoaks. He had no idea what this Janet looked like, and just hoped that when she inevitably wanted to sleep with him that he would be able to superimpose Megan Fox's face and body onto her for the whole thing using just the power of his incredible mind. He had on his lovely new shiny tracksuit tucked into silver cowboy boots, and had beautifully brushed his ponytail, the only problem he might encounter (apart from having to sleep with a possible munter) was trying to keep all the other women from pouncing and ruining the date.

"Hello Stephen".

He turned around, and saw a woman who would actually have been considered attractive, if she was younger. She was slim, well-dressed, and classy-looking, and he thought she had the look of Charlize Theron's slightly-older sister. Perhaps if I have a little alcohol I can do my bit for charity after all and help the aged, he thought to himself.

"Hello, you must be Janet".

The Unbearable Heaviness of Stephen Seagull.

"Yes, I'm so excited to meet you at last Stephen, I'm a huge fan".

"Well, who isn't?"

"No- one of any consequence. So would you like to go in for some breakfast?"

"Does Jet Li bow down at a massive poster of me every night before going to bed?"

"Um, I've absolutely no idea who that is Stephen".

"Yes, I would like to go in for some more breakfast".

They entered the hotel, Big Stevie walking a little behind so he could have a look at her aged arse. Not bad, he thought, all things considered. They went and sat in the dining area, where she ordered a light breakfast for herself and he ordered the same, twice, in a big bap. With chips. And a side order of more chips.

"So, what is it about me that you like so much then, apart from the obvious looks, charisma, manliness, acting skills, powerful rippling physique, brooding intensity, intelligence, humour, script-writing, directing, producing, athleticism, ponytail, fighting skills, tasteful guitar-playing, soulful singing, charity work, and quiet understated dignity?"

"I'm not sure there's anything left Stephen, I think you've covered it all. I've just always really loved your films, I'm a sucker for some mindless violence and big, beefy men battering the hell out of each other for an hour and a half".

"Well I think you'll find there's more to my films than just mindless violence Janet, I'm always layering them with subtle subtext and hidden meaning. For instance Anvil in Your Mother's Face may have looked, on the face of it, just to be about a family feud that escalated into all-out war that reduced a small town to rubble, but it was actually about religious intolerance".

"Can you explain it to me a little Stephen, I missed that when I watched the countless scenes of people throwing their grannies into woodchippers and nephews impaling uncles on pitchforks".

"Look do I have to spell it out for you? when Krank cut Maallingham's genitals off and force-fed them to his own grandfather it was clearly a critique of Christian dogma, and if you couldn't see that then you really are as thick as two short planks covered in pig-shit, and there is no hope for you. No offence".

"None taken...and when Bergron buggers Jegson while drinking moonshine and playing Poison's Talk Dirty To Me on his banjo?"

"Obviously that was about Islamic extremism".

"Could you explain to me in layman's terms?"

"Look Janet no offence but I didn't come here to talk about me; so tell me, what do you do?"

"I own my own retail business with shops all over the UK, and thanks to some wise investments from the profits I need never work again, but I enjoy the challenge of it all".

The Unbearable Heaviness of Stephen Seagull.

"That's great. Anyway my film career is going from strength to strength, and I should be finished my latest album once I get back to LA and do the mixes. I hesitate to say this as it may sound a bit cocky, but I think it might be the best album of all time, and will change the face of music".

"I haven't actually listened to any of your music Stephen, sorry. I'm not really into music to be honest, I'm more of a film person".

"That's fair enough, but I guarantee that if you listened to MY music the scales would fall from your eyes and you would be a born-again music lover. Ha! Scales, music! I've just made a hilarious joke and I'm so clever I did it without even realising! Perhaps I should add stand-up comedy to my list of talents".

"Perhaps…Anyway I might have a listen sometime, maybe look up some of your stuff online".

"You should come and see me live if you want to experience my music as it really should be experienced. People have described it as almost religious, and that up on that stage I almost glow with spiritual essence. Some cynics say it's just the spotlights on the stage, but my fans know better".

"I would love to Stephen. So I take it that there's no-one special in your life at the moment?"

"No, not that I can think of. I do live with someone but she's just a maid, pretty much. I'm not actually looking for a relationship at the moment though anyway, I'm happy being a lone wolf". This wasn't entirely true, if some sexy young woman came along he would be totally up for it, but he thought that it was best to knock any ideas that this reasonably attractive but old woman had of perhaps getting into a long-term relationship with him on the head.

"Maybe I can change that line of thought Stephen, I'm confident that by the end of this weekend you will have fallen hopelessly in love with me, and want to settle down into a happy marriage and live happily ever after".

"No, sorry, that isn't going to happen. Look don't take this the wrong way but I can see me probably sleeping with you after a few drinks this weekend, but as for anything long term you're just not what I'm looking for, sorry".

"And what exactly is that then? I mean, without wishing to blow my own trumpet I think I look pretty good. I've kept myself in shape, I don't think I'm unattractive, I dress well, so why am I such a straight no?"

"To be brutally honest, you're just too old for me".

She burst out laughing.

"Stephen! I'm eleven years younger than you!"

"I very much doubt that".

"It's true Stephen, remember I'm a huge fan of yours so I know pretty much everything about you including your date of birth".

"Well regardless, you're still too old for me, I'm a major film star; I don't have to settle for a woman who is past her best. No offence again".

111

The Unbearable Heaviness of Stephen Seagull.

"Some taken. Come on though Stephen get real, a young beautiful woman is going to be far more interested in a young, handsome film star than someone like you who, who, no offence, is a bit past your best".

"What the hell are you talking about woman? I'm in my absolute prime! Any woman would be delighted to snare a hunky specimen of masculine perfection like me".

"Stephen, you know I look at you and see a handsome elder statesman, and I would go out with you like a shot, but looking at you objectively as say a young woman who knows nothing about you might look at you, then it's safe to say that what SHE might see is a morbidly-obese, piggy-eyed, humourless, decrepit old oaf who clearly dyes his ridiculous ponytail and goatee".

"Are you sure you're a fan?"

"Stephen, I'm just saying that if you come down into reality then what you have in front of you is an attractive, willing woman who could bring you happiness and love, if you could just get over your fixation with chasing women half your age. On that note remember that I am still eleven years younger".

"Nice try Grandma but I think I'll stick to pulling hot young babes thanks, though I might let you sleep with me later if you play your cards right, and I've had enough to drink".

"Oh Stephen, what are you like?" She sighed, and gave up the conversation. They spent the rest of the day together, and went for drinks all over London that night. They had a lot of fun and Big Stevie enjoyed her company, surprisingly, and was sorry when the end drew near.

"So, will you come back to the hotel for a nightcap Stephen?"

"Alright then, I suppose a couple more drinks won't hurt".

She helped lift him out of the taxi, and they went to her room at the hotel.

"Now, let's see what the minibar has for us".

She poured them both a large whisky and they sat on the bed.

As he sat on the edge of the bed desperately trying to hold his stomachs in (along with a potentially potent fart), he was feeling woozy. He had been careful to watch his alcohol intake over the course of the day, not because he couldn't handle his drink (he wasn't a pussy), but just in case any of the meals he had eaten over the past few weeks disagreed with him again. Although he was feeling a bit giddy the booze was making him feel a bit horny, and as he looked at the old woman he felt a stirring in his loins, as well as his guts.

"I've had a really great time tonight Stephen, I loved hearing all of your stories about fighting in Korea, World War Two, or WW2 if that's how you like to say it, Vietnam, the Gulf war and countless other warzones; you really have been everywhere and done everything, even though your timelines may seem to the untrained eye to be somewhat confusing, and to lesser eyes bullshit".

"To masters like me time has no meaning, we are everywhere at every time, all-seeing, all-eating".

The Unbearable Heaviness of Stephen Seagull.

A small parp escaped his arse-cheeks, but he was confident that a hasty cough had covered it up satisfactorily.

"Well master, as time has no meaning then perhaps age doesn't either? Maybe you can ditch your silly ageism when it comes to partners and see what a good thing you have in front of you".

"Maybe a little test drive tonight and then see how it goes..."

"You old smoothie...but okay then, you had me at hello. Let's put a lovely layer of icing onto today's nice cake and...oh my god, what the hell is that smell?"

"I can't smell it...oh wait yes, I think I do detect a faint aroma".

"A faint aroma? It smells like someone has filled a skip full of rancid fish, had a herd of buffalo shit on top of it, and then left it out for two weeks at the height of summer".

"I think perhaps there might be a dead rat in an air vent or something, maybe we should call down to the front desk".

"Oh god, talk about a passion killer, my olfactory system has gone on strike".

"Yes, my ofalactory system has too, it's awful".

She got up and grabbed a bottle of perfume from the top of a bedside cabinet, and sprayed it liberally all around the room, gagging slightly as she did so. After almost emptying the bottle the room was thick with a slightly-sickly sweet perfume cloud, and a faint hint of something far more faecal lingering underneath.

"That's better" he said, getting up from the bed with a loud grunt. "Now on a completely unrelated note, I have to use the little boy's room, so I'll just be a minute. I don't suppose you have a newspaper in here, do you?"

"No Stephen, I don't".

"Never mind, I have my phone with me".

He went into the bathroom, closed the door, he took out his phone, initially to have a look at some young women on the internet to get him in the mood for later, but then decided that some music might be a better idea to mask any occasional embarrassing noises that may leak out of the room over the next twenty minutes.

For the next twenty (plus an additional 12...) minutes Janet sat on the bed idly staring at the wall in front of her as the sounds of AC/DC's Back in Black album came through the wall, interspersed with what sounded like someone dropping furniture out of a plane into a lake while thunder rumbled. This soundtrack was embellished now and again by what sounded like the noises a female elephant might make while giving birth, followed by loud panting, gasping and muttered swearwords. Eventually she heard the toilet flush and waited for him to come back out. Nothing. After a minute or two she heard the toilet flush again but still no sign of the door opening. She pondered whether to call out to him, but after another minute or two she heard the toilet flushing again, a muttered "oh thank fuck", and then

The Unbearable Heaviness of Stephen Seagull.

Big Stevie exited the bathroom, closing the door quickly behind him. Unfortunately not quite quick enough, and Janet's eyes instantly began to water furiously, and her nostrils tried to close of their own accord.

"Sorry" Big Stevie said, pulling up his tracksuit bottoms. "I thought I would just give my teeth a little brush before bed".

"Yes...that's an interesting flavour of toothpaste I can smell".

"It's my own brand, spearmint with a few spices added for a little extra kick".

"Well it certainly does kick Stephen, like a mule on steroids".

"Now" he smiled, as he laid back down on the bed beside her, "where were we?".

She cursed inwardly at having only brought one bottle of perfume with her. She thought about sticking some toothpaste up her nostrils to try and block out the smell, but there was no way that she was going in THERE. She would just have to try and foil evolution and biology and quickly learn to breathe through her ears, and soldier on.

"I'll put on some suitable music" Big Stevie said, looking through his phone, as she dimmed the lights in the room romantically. After a minute another AC/DC song, Let's Get It Up, blasted out of his phone, and he unzipped the top of his tracksuit sexily.

"So baby, let's make some magic together" he wheezed, struggling with the effort of holding his gut in. He put his feet up onto the bed and motioned for her to take his boots off, as there was no way he was ever going to be able to bend down there without another parp escaping his arse.

She removed his boots and socks, and began to strip seductively. He pulled his tracksuit bottoms down, shimmying them down past his arse cheeks not quite so seductively. A part of him was wishing that he hadn't had that curry n' chips n' curry n' chips so near to the end of the night, and he could feel his stomach making some quite unpleasant noises as he pulled down his Spiderman long johns.

She lay her naked body on top of him ("don't press on my guts, don't press on my guts"), and slowly undid his corset. Without its help the strain of holding his stomachs in was too much for Big Stevie, and his belly flew out with such force that it struck her hard in the face, knocking her across the room and into the minbar.

"Shit, are you okay?" He said worriedly, heaving himself off the bed and waddling over to her.

"Y...yes...I'm okay Stephen...my head hurts a bit, but I should be okay in a minute or two".

In his rush to aid her a small parp had escaped again, and even Big Stevie gagged a little at this one.

"So, where were we, mon amour?" he said in his best Barry White growl, hoping to get quickly back to the business in hand and distract her from the pungent aroma that was burning his nostrils going in almost as much as it had burned his arsehole going out.

"Stephen I...JESUS H CHRIST! There's that unholy reek again! Was that you Stephen? Oh my god, my eyes, my nose". Her hand rose to her face, covering it as she gagged repeatedly. She rushed into the

114

The Unbearable Heaviness of Stephen Seagull.

toilet but just as quickly rushed back out again, and suddenly, without warning, she was sick all over his Spiderman long johns lying there on the bedroom floor.

"Oh god, I'm sorry, Stephen" she gasped, holding both her stomach and her nose. "but that smell…"

"I can't smell it" he lied, red eyes watering as he breathed through his mouth. "So, where were we?"

He moved towards her and placed a hand on her body, but she moved away.

"I think the moment has gone Stephen, maybe we should call it a night".

"But I've still got a semi!"

"And I still have a pounding head from where your gargantuan guts threw me across the room, and stinging eyeballs and nostrils from when your fart turned the air brown".

"A quick hand job then?"

"Just go Stephen".

"Fine, your loss".

He began putting his clothes back on, wondering briefly whether to steal her discarded bra for later wanking purposes, but decided against it. As he bent over to put on his cowboy boots he felt his belly churning once more, and it took all of his willpower to keep everything under control.

"Goodnight Stephen" she said, still lying on the floor, holding her head, "I think we'll give tomorrow a miss".

"Oh, alright then, fair enough". He turned towards the door, but then his guts began to churn uncomfortably again. "Um, any chance I can use your toilet again before I go?"

The Unbearable Heaviness of Stephen Seagull.

Big Stevie had decided that he didn't want to see Janet anymore, as she was too old. He had tried to give her a chance that night as he wasn't shallow, but she wasn't for him. It didn't matter anyway, as there were plenty more fish in the sea for a sexy mother Hubbard like him, and worst come to the worst he still had a wife at home.

Master of Warriors opened to mixed reviews ("the tiny budget is most apparent during the gunfights, when the thugs shouting BANG BANG every time they fire takes you out of the film somewhat-The Manchester Monocle; "Like taking a cheese grater to your testicles and eating the gratings with urine gravy"-The Dundee Infidel; "It was bad enough that the bank holdup was clearly filmed in a taxi cab office, but they could at least have stopped taking fares on the phones in the background of the scenes"-The Sussex Monkeyspungler), but it was the number two film one Tuesday in a cinema in a small village not far from Cardiff.

Big Stevie decided that it was time to go back home and see um...Susan...yes, that was it. She seemed really pleased to see him (and sunlight) when he unlocked her from the house, and in a funny way he missed her a little bit too; no-one rubbed his bunions like she did. Perhaps he had taken this mid-twenties, slender, attractive, and competent cleaner and cooker for granted, maybe he should make more of an effort to see if she was actual partner material. The language barrier was a problem of course, but he had already paid for her to do an English course to improve that, and given her a very reasonable interest rate on the loan payback plan.

He had entered a good phase in his life: he was still in his physical prime, still had the looks of a twenty-nine-year-old stud, a long, luxurious and not-at-all dyed ponytail, some attractive arm-candy for a wife, and his films still made money. Technically this is not necessarily the same as "profit", but they made money. He was incredibly excited about his new idea for a film script: Rogue Cobbler, about a man, Bolt Gaarson, who runs a shoe-repair and key-cutting service in Los Angeles, but is in fact a retired SAS Navy Seal Marine. The local mafia are demanding protection money from all the shops on his street and have done for years, and Bolt has been complying for a quiet life, but then a young single mother opens up a beauty salon and runs into debt paying off the goons. This will mean that her really cute, telegenic children will be taken away from her by the authorities and sold for scrap, unless she can find a way to find the money. Oh yes, and she looks after her dear old pensioner father, a retired police chief and decorated war hero, who lost the use of his elbows and the back of his neck during 'Nam. Bolt finds this out, and decides that it is finally time to take out the trash. Then after that he will fight the mafia.

He takes out his guitar, an idea already forming for the theme song, and begins to note down some lyrics:

"From the East came a mighty warrior,

Tall and strong and bold,

If he has a migraine he will tough it right out,

And laughs in the face of a cold.

Powerful and muscular, patriotic and mysterious,

His ponytail infused with the power of the gods.

116

The Unbearable Heaviness of Stephen Seagull.

No matter the nationality of the thugs he is fighting,

He will always manage to even the odds.

A friend to the chicks and a foe to the bad,

A righter of wrongs and destroyer of evil.

Quietly mysterious and broodily handsome,

His spiritual animal would be the weevil.

He can punch through walls and kick through cars,

A one-man army who will bring bad guys to their knees.

An aura of danger mixed with a halo of hope,

Who'll also do your shoes and cut your keys".

It was just a rough, off-the-top-of-his-head idea at the moment, but he already had a feeling that this might turn out to be one of the best four songs of all time, and certainly the best film soundtrack.

He lay down the guitar and walked over to his wardrobe. Searching around for the right uniform for his character he eventually found what he was looking for, and stood in front of the mirror with a smile. As he put on the Native American head-dress and leather waistcoat he was already almost Bolt, key-cutter extraordinaire, but there was just one more item: he reached into the waistcoat pocket and dug out the sunglasses. There, that was it, when people came into the shoe repair shop and looked at this man they would just know that while he seemed like any other pleasant and amiable shopkeeper, that there was an element of danger that hinted at a lot more backstory to this rugged stranger.

The film was barely a sketch at this moment in time, and the theme tune a few strummed chords and hastily-scribbled lyrics, but already he felt an excitement he hadn't felt about a project in a long, long time. As he walked through to the kitchen to look for the takeaway menu he felt that this was going to be the year when things went back to how they should be again, and the world once more realised that he was a stone-cold legend, and send Rogue Cobbler to number one in the film charts all over the world.

He picked up his guitar again, and began to quietly sing an idea for the chorus:

Rogue cobbler, he'll kick you in the bum,

Rogue cobbler, but he'll never hurt your mum,

Rogue cobbler, he's sexy but he's dangerous,

Rogue cobbler, Jean Claude Van Damme is just so envious,

Rogue cobbler, his prices are very reasonable,

Rogue cobbler, he can't think of a rhyme for reasonable,

Rogue cobbler, your keys will be ready in half an hour,

The Unbearable Heaviness of Stephen Seagull.

Rogue cobbler, for lunch today he's having sweet and sour.

My god this masterpiece writes itself he thought with a grin, as he thought about the likelihood of getting both an Oscar AND a platinum album out of this epic. He felt so good about his prospects that the decided it was time to treat himself to a celebratory wank, and logged onto his favourite free porn site, and entered "Brazilian midget granny porn" into the search box. He reached into the bedside drawer and dug out crusty, his old faithful wanking sock, and clicked onto the first vid that took his fancy. As he got down to business he hoped Susan was going to be a while yet digging the foundations for the new conservatory, and he wouldn't be interrupted.

As he lay there, a slight smile tracing across his lips, right arm pumping like an electric sewing machine needle, ideas for Rogue Cobbler flooded his brain (there definitely would NOT be any small foreign pensioners doing THAT in Rogue Cobbler though, and he must really strive harder to separate his thoughts for the film and the images on the screen in front of him). This was going to be the one that got him right back on top, and, if all else failed, there was always Trapped On A Big Ship 3.

Printed in Great Britain
by Amazon